**BUILD
UNIVERSES**

To Thomas,
I hope you
enjoy the book.
Steve Morris

Steve Morris

The Distant Beat

europe books

© 2020 **Europe Books**
europe-books.co.uk

ISBN 979-12-201-0267-4
First edition: October 2020

The Distant Beat

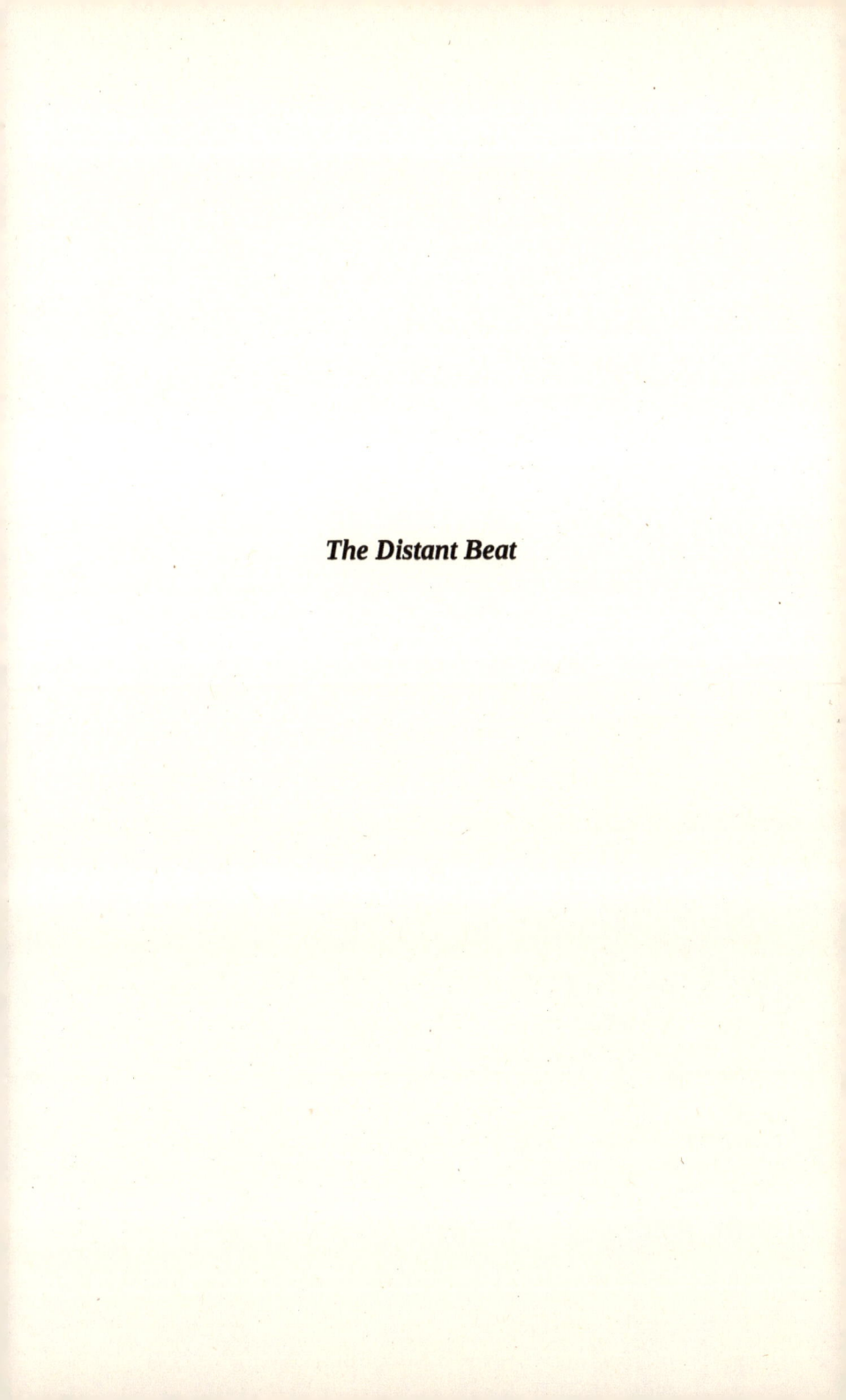

For Ellie and Joe

Contents

Chapter 1	11
Chapter 2	23
Chapter 3	33
Chapter 4	43
Chapter 5	57
Chapter 6	69
Chapter 7	81
Chapter 8	89
Chapter 9	99
Chapter 10	107
Chapter 11	119
Chapter 12	133
Chapter 13	143
Chapter 14	155

CHAPTER 1

The last six weeks had flown by and without question, this was Danny Bowen's favourite summer. For the first time he could ever recall, he was bursting with excitement and anticipation, just a week away from starting his last year in primary school.

For a good while, Danny had decided that he wasn't cut out for school but all of that had changed just two months earlier, when he arrived in Shropshire and first set eyes on Northernvale Primary School. Nestled in the heart of Northernvale itself, it was a picture-postcard village and even at that stage, he knew there was something different about this place. To start with, he'd not experienced that same old sinking feeling when arriving at his latest primary school. Four schools in two years! The same routine of hurriedly packing and moving on at little or no notice.

"It's the last time my love, I hope…" would be the tired old line his mother would utter as she turned the key in the car ignition; setting off for the latest place of refuge and safety. The difference this time, was the sheer contrast. And it was that contrast which filled Danny with a different and more positive feeling. His mum felt it too.

Leaving Liverpool, crammed with the sounds of any urban sprawl was always going to be very, very different. However, different was good, as far as Danny was concerned. Different was necessary. He and his mother were inseparable but whilst there had been happy moments, positive memories hardly flowed from Danny's home city. His mum was overprotective – this was understandable when you considered that Danny's dad was someone to be avoided, rather than cherished and kept close.

Now all of that was behind them, Danny had noticed that his mum had looked much less tired than he could ever recall. He put that down to this most recent of moves.

Danny's experience of Northernvale Primary actually totalled no more than the six weeks of the school holidays he had just enjoyed off. This was due to him having arrived in Shropshire during the first week of June. Not only would he be returning to school as a year 6 pupil, he'd also be in Miss Patel's class again. Miss Patel was like another mum to Danny. She was kind. She understood. She was different and Danny was determined to repay her faith in him, by doing the right thing more often and giving it his all – even in History, his least favourite subject.

Toby and Delilah (Danny's best mates) were also in Miss Patel's class. Another reason to look forward to the new term, despite the fact he'd spent most of the summer with them, out on the village green; the three of them on their bikes and living in each other's pockets.

The final day of his summer holidays had been dominated by the *'dreaded'* new school shoes shop. Normally a potential flashpoint it had gone surprisingly smoothly this time. Another positive sign from his mother's perspective.

New school shoes or not, Danny sprinted the hundred metres or so from his front door to the playground entrance on the first day of the new school year. If truth be known, he had been awake since dawn - woken by the early morning chorus of birds, perilously perched on the swaying branches of the silver birch, outside his bedroom window. Danny's latest house was even older than the school itself - a tired, slightly unloved two-up, two-down - in desperate need of a lick of paint. It was accompanied with a small, featureless garden which overlooked the playground on which l now standing.

"New shoes, Danny?" came the voice from behind him, "you're not the only one today – look!"

By this point, Danny had swivelled around to be greeted by a smiling Miss Patel, who was also sporting brand new shoes.

"Good summer, Miss?" enquired Danny.

"It was lovely, thank you. And yours?"

"Yeah, not bad at all Miss, thanks – 'cept these new shoes are rubbing a bit and I've only had them on for a couple of minutes!"

The playground niceties were interrupted as the bell sounded and the crowds of milling parents and children bade farewell to each other, with a mix of kisses, waves and hair-ruffling. Danny spotted Toby and latched onto the back of the class line. He didn't mind his mum not accompanying him the short distance to school; after all, he was grown up enough to take care of getting himself to school in the morning and back home, at the end of each day. In class, Miss Patel allowed the first day hubbub of chatter to fill the opening five minutes, as classmates used the opportunity to catch up after a long summer away. As a gradual hush descended over the children, Miss Patel addressed the members of Wrekin Class. Just ahead of the 9.30AM assembly, she distributed the first of the year 6 monitor jobs. Danny and Toby were installed as the *'Assembly Monitors'*.

"Now, I shouldn't need to remind you boys but you need to ensure that the music is on as classes file into assembly; that chairs are out for the adults and the benches are placed at the back of the hall for the year 6s."

"Yes Miss… thanks Miss… can we do it now, Miss?" requested Toby. Toby loved jobs and responsibilities and little had changed over the summer.

Within a minute, both boys had hurried down the corridor and were busying themselves with the job in hand. Without really noticing, Mr Stanley, the school's headteacher, made his way into the school hall. After a cheery welcome, he posed a peculiar question.

"What does a century mean to you, Toby?"

After a degree of hesitation, Toby finally replied.

"Well... my great-grandad is nearly a century old, Mr Stanley, I think he's ninety-four!"

"Pretty good answer, Toby. I do hope your great-grandad is in good health but it's not just people who clock up a century, it's buildings too. Boys, this is your last year in this school and by coincidence, it's also our school's 100th birthday!"

"So, does that mean we get a day off school?" interrupted Danny, with one of his typical quips.

"Not quite Danny but we will need to organise a wonderful birthday party for this place," as he raised an eyebrow to indicate the hall and the building in which they stood.

After a pause, Toby asked if his great-grandad could attend the celebration and was delighted when Mr Stanley responded by suggesting that it sounded like a good idea. By now the hall had begun to fill with pupils from the school's five classes – ranging from the brand-new Reception pupils, through to year 6, as well as all of the staff. The old, imposing school building had grown over time to accommodate the increasing number of pupils and it had never been larger, having had two extensions in more recent years.

As the boys suspected, Mr Stanley's *'Welcome Back'* assembly focused on the school's rapidly-approaching centenary. The big day was set for Friday, 1st July – a long way off but as Mr Stanley explained, there was much to do. Each of the five classes were given an area of responsibility in preparation for *'Northernvale's Centenary Celebrations'*. The younger classes were to arrange the costumes, party food, games and decorations but much of the organisation was to fall to Wrekin Class. Toby's conversation and request of Mr Stanley for his great-grandad to attend, meant the class were responsible for the VIP list! One hundred grand guests, one VIP for each year that the school had stood in the heart of the village.

"Of course…" explained Miss Patel, when back in class, "this special day will see even more guests but our job is to identify and invite one hundred 'VIGers' *(Very Important Guests)* as I'd like to call them."

"Aargh but that's really boring, why can't we do something else?" protested Lucy. Lucy always protested, even when there was little or nothing to protest about. Skilfully ignoring her, Miss Patel added, "And it's important that our very own century of invited guests all have a strong link with our school. This afternoon we'll begin to think about how we can achieve this."

The rest of the school week flew by – Miss Patel wasn't especially impressed with class suggestions around the one hundred 'VIGers' but Ellie Cooper told all those who'd listen, that Miss Patel would do it for them anyway. Delilah felt that Ellie did have a point, stating that the first of July was so far off. Of course, there was some truth in this and as the school year slowly ticked by, week upon week, there was no real urgency.

Even as the horse chestnut tree - overhanging the school field – shed its bounty of conkers, little progress was made. Reverend Williams arrived with harvest and prayers of thankfulness on her mind; whilst parents dug out the heavier winter coats for the autumn, squeezing their children into them, wondering if the coat could manage another four months of wear.

It was one of those conkers, bouncing painfully off the back of Danny's head, that reminded him that kindness and friendship was not important to all pupils, especially so in the case of Millie and Mattie Doubty. Millie and Mattie were non-identical twins but both had behaved identically towards Danny since his arrival the previous June. Just their presence alone brought Danny's mood down and tested his patience. Despite sharing his frustration and worries with Miss Patel, some things definitely hadn't changed since before the summer. To further complicate the situation, they happened to live next door to Danny, so it was often difficult to put any sort of distance between himself and them. Danny's disputes with the duo had been verbal so far and he was determined to keep it that way. Too often in his past, he'd made wrong choices when faced with conflict and had frequently resorted to using his feet and fists to solve his problems. He would often regret it afterwards and was well aware, more than anybody else, that he needed to better manage his emotions. So, tolerating others was certainly something Danny was getting better at and with his least-favourite twins in the world living so close, he was getting plenty of practice!

With a more settled and predictable life – minus Millie and Mattie – Danny was able to better appreciate his surroundings and the rural setting, he felt, helped to keep his emotions in check. For the first time, he gained pleasure from the other seasons, not just the summer. From the light morning frost and dew on the ground to the gentle fading of colour and life from the leaves on the trees, autumn was most definitely here. The rustic reds and golden shades were beautiful in their own way, providing a kaleidoscope of colour and the fresh northerly wind was something Danny embraced more readily these days, rather than wrapping up and turning his back on it. However, it was those unpredictable and heavy autumn showers that Danny wasn't prepared to change his viewpoint on. They were frustrating, never more so than when it meant a wet break or dinnertime.

It was one of those dinnertimes when the topic of conversation turned to the upcoming Halloween disco.

"So what costume are you gonna wear, Danny?" asked Delilah.

"Not too bothered to be honest. It's for the younger kids anyway – everyone knows that," he replied.

"Well, my mum and dad are going to a Halloween party and they're thirty-nine and forty, so that makes no sense!" retorted Delilah.

"S'pose I will be going but seeing as it's early October, I'm not gonna worry about it," Danny added firmly, hoping that that would bring an end to the conversation.

"You don't really need to make much effort with a costume, to be honest, Danny..." added Millie, nastily. She was the master of eavesdropping and this unwelcome offering came with an unpleasant smirk, too.

"Danny's table – back to work, please!" demanded Miss Patel.

That afternoon dragged a little but the prospect of after-school football practice kept Danny going. He didn't mind football. He wasn't an especially good player but that didn't deter him. Danny was the type of boy who would turn his hand to anything, especially if it involved the outdoors and ideally took place in the summer when the sun was meant to shine. Whilst his friends were forever talking about their latest exploits on their games consoles, Danny had never really got it and also didn't want to be pestering his mother for something he knew she could never afford to buy him.

The following week was a crucial one for Wrekin Class – preparations for the school's centenary day were taking shape elsewhere and Miss Patel knew it.

"We really need to come up with a plan this week, Wrekin Class! I can tell you that staff have been sharing progress in other classes and I'd like to join in with those conversations, thank you very much!"

The class knew Miss Patel meant business, so that afternoon they set to work. As the end-of-school bell sounded, their teacher was able to dismiss the class with a good degree of satisfaction, ahead of marching into the lower key stage two classroom, next door.

"Well, Mr Fowler, we've made progress, I'm pleased to report!" stated Miss Patel in a very grand manner.

"Wonderful…" replied Mr Fowler, "please do tell me more."

It was true. The children had enjoyed an extremely productive afternoon, designing an attractive invitation as well as identifying over thirty more VIGers. The list included: governors (past and present); former teachers at the school; a handful of local councillors and even the local MP. At last, things were beginning to shape up. Even so, they were still well short of their one hundred guest target, set by Mr Stanley.

The following day was equally as productive, with Toby suggesting the school ought to invite anybody over one hundred – or in their nineties – who were still living in, or near the village, to be one of the VIGers so as to keep his great-grandad company. The class and Miss Patel were in agreement. However, it was the class teaching assistant, Mrs Owen, who made the most valuable contribution, suggesting that old school records – most probably safely stored in the loft - should be unearthed so as to shed light on any other people from the past who the school could contact.

So, it was Wrekin Class's teaching assistant who was charged with retrieving any relevant documents from the loft and being marginally past her prime, she requested the assistance of Danny and Delilah to help her with this quest.

"Don't worry you two, the school loft floor was partially boarded many years ago, before even I had started at Northernvale!" stated Mrs Owen with a smile, as she placed her foot securely on the bottom rung of the ladder. A minute later she was out of sight but beckoned Danny and Delilah to follow her lead. Moments later they were clambering off the top of the step ladder and into the loft. Both pupils were taken aback by the sheer size of the space, as well as the volume of objects scattered around in a manner which suggested items were routinely deposited into the loft in something of a hurry. The majority of these unidentified objects were cloaked in enormous dust sheets which further complicated matters, as it was difficult to make out the actual dimension and shape of many of the concealed items.

As their eyes became accustomed to the dim light, they figured that the space was more than big enough to house all the pupils in Wrekin Class! The loft's structure replicated the grand V-shaped eaves at the front of the building, the oldest section of the school and according to Mrs Owen, the original staffroom. She went on to explain that a small wooden flight of stairs had provided access to the space but these had been demolished some sixty years previously.

"I'd love to be a fly on the wall in our staffroom, Mrs Owen," laughed Delilah as she made her way over to one of the darkest recesses of the loft.

"Just take a look in the corner you're heading towards, Delilah. Danny, can you search over there?" Mrs Owen added, whilst pointing into a corner which was marginally better lit, due to a mossy, sky light which was blanketed in a film of dirt and grime.

"There's so much up here, Miss, can't we just organise a human chain and empty the loft?" asked Danny. This made little sense to Mrs Owen as she knew what she was looking for, so simply encouraged the duo to continue looking.

A short while later, maybe no more than ten minutes, a head popped up through the open loft hatch.

"Any luck up there?" boomed Mr Stanley, trying hard to peer through the dimly-lit environment. "We really should've got this space hooked up with electricity a long time ago."

"Aha!" exclaimed Mrs Owen, almost simultaneously, "success, I believe!"

Both Danny and Delilah, backs hunched, abandoned their searches to find Mrs Owen crouched over a large, sealed cardboard box with the phrase: 'School Records/Log Books 1919 to 1939', printed neatly on the top of the box. As she blew and wiped the dust clear off the tops of four other similar boxes nearby, she noticed the contents of these boxes indicated that they'd found school records which took the school up to and beyond the year 2000.

"Just the job!" announced Mrs Owen, unable to disguise the delight in her voice.

"Super work, the three of you, let's get them out of here and down to Wrekin Class then," added Mr Stanley, who had by now, also ventured up into the loft.

The intrepid trio – along with Mr Stanley – were greeted like returning heroes as they each strode into class, with the boxes. Miss Patel responded by handing out three house points to Danny and Delilah. In her excitement she presented Mrs Owen and Mr Stanley with the same reward, much to the delight and entertainment of the class.

This was only the start of the hard work though. Every afternoon for the next week involved each table in class poring over the documents, with a view to uncovering interesting facts about the school as well as unearthing the identity of other potential VIGers to invite to the party.

With Mr Stanley's blessing, that last week before half-term saw the entire class inspecting their own box, in minute detail. The weekly PE slot came and went, with no PE lesson! However, even Danny didn't bat an eyelid, let alone complain. Almost half of the class asked Miss Patel for permission to work through their lunchtimes – a worthwhile pursuit as the week concluded with Wrekin Class gathering more information than they, or even Miss Patel, knew what to do with. Without realising, the class had slowly but surely pieced together a potted history of the school for its entire ninety-nine-year existence.

So, what next, class?" asked Miss Patel with a contented smile, on that final Friday afternoon.

"Well Miss, I'm not gonna spend my half-term looking through old family documents!" quipped Joe. The class responded with laughter, to which Miss Patel simply repeated her original question.

"S'pose we should work out the most important information we've found and then work out how we use it to track down even more people to invite," summarised Delilah, very succinctly.

"Sounds like a plan…" Miss Patel added, before pausing, "and you can all relax over the half-term – leave it with me."

The challenge Miss Patel had accepted on behalf of the children was an unenviable one. The pupils had, by the class's estimation, already identified the names of up to sixty more VIGers who might still live locally and crucially, still be alive!

"I take my hat off to you and your class, Miss Patel. You've really upped your game," conceded Mr Fowler, over the staff buffet that Friday afternoon. To top off the half-term, Mr Stanley used that afternoon's *'Awards Assembly'* to present a certificate to all members of Wrekin Class. Citing their *'determination and application when completing historical research for our centenary celebrations'*, he happily handed over the certificate to Millie Doubty, who

Miss Patel had nominated to collect it on behalf of the whole class. Even Danny had to concede that she too had worked really hard throughout that final week.

"Please don't forget..." continued Mr Stanley, as the assembly reached its conclusion, "that the school doors will be open from 6pm this evening, for our Halloween Disco. I hope to see as many of you there, as possible." Shortly afterwards, the classes filed quietly out of assembly and then, after collecting reading books and PE kits, home.

CHAPTER 2

Fancy dress, including scary outfits, were optional. So, when Toby called at Danny's that evening in a full-on werewolf outfit, Danny wondered how many small children he must have frightened half to death, in the ten-minute walk between the two houses! Danny's mum wasn't going to let him attend without a costume – especially as she'd spent all of that afternoon fashioning an old white bedsheet into a more than passable ghost outfit, adorned with ghoulish eyes and a terrifying, black hole of a mouth which Danny acknowledged looked pretty cool. So, there they were – a ghost and a werewolf, off to the school disco.

"D'you know what, Danny? We look great!" grinned Toby from behind his mask, as they entered the school hall.

Staff had done a fantastic job of converting the hall into a Halloween-themed disco: candle-lit pumpkins, miniature ghosts, broomsticks, cauldrons and witches galore – it had the lot. The next ninety minutes flew by with all, including Mr Stanley - dressed as a vampire - having a great time. As the last song faded away, Danny said his goodbyes to Toby and Delilah before heading home.

Of course, it was only a thirty second walk but that was enough of an opportunity for the twins to strike! From behind a neighbour's gate, Mattie Doubty jumped out on Danny.

"Trick or treat, Bowen?"

"Neither, go home Mattie!" replied Danny, dismissively.

Before he could react, Mattie bellowed *'trick'*, lunged forward and shoved Danny in the chest. As Danny careered backwards, ghoul number two, Millie, stuck her foot out, causing Danny to lose balance and land heavily in a heap. As the twins raced home, Danny picked himself up and realising that both elbows were bleeding, dusted himself down before continuing home. Whilst upset, he didn't want to burden his mum with this further episode. So, he crept upstairs and cleaned the blood from his arms before changing into his pyjamas. Revenge would be his but he figured he'd have to be patient.

The following evening, Danny's mum ordered a rare takeaway pizza, as they both curled up on the sofa in front of a film. She had insisted on treating her son, particularly as she had a little money left at the end of the month, rather than none at all. Putting the twins to the back of his mind, he paused the television and turned towards his mother. "Mum, please tell me that we won't be moving again. This has been the best two months I've ever had at school. I love this school and even this house. I want to stay in Northernvale, more than anything else. Can we stay? Will we stay?"

Danny's mum smiled and gave him a hug. She hoped for the same but knew, sadly, that she couldn't guarantee what he was asking for, so changed the subject.

"If you continue to behave so well and try so hard at school for the rest of the year, as you have done for the last two months, then I'll be the proudest mum in the world!"

With that, she planted a kiss on Danny's forehead and pressed the play button. They watched the remainder of the film in silence.

The beginning of the half term holiday started slowly. Danny's mum had managed to secure occasional hours at the local one-stop store and he enjoyed the independence and responsibility that came with taking care of himself. For Danny, it was another green light from his mother that he was maturing and growing into a young man who could be trusted. In addition, she was only a two-minute jog from home, if required, not to mention on the other end of her mobile phone.

With both Delilah and Toby away for the week, it was times like this that Danny would have loved a younger, or older, sibling to play with. However, he'd got used to it being just the two of them and with the recent disruption in his life he found it hard to imagine a third member of the family needing to be looked after.

On the Wednesday of that week, with his mum on a three-hour shift, Danny headed absent-mindedly into the garden and began to kick his football around. He had previously managed seventeen keepy-ups, so set about improving his *'all-time'* record. Before long though, his concentration was side-tracked by a monumental storm, where leaden-grey clouds quickly formed before his very eyes, ahead of depositing what Danny thought was close to a year's supply of rain directly onto him! Where most would run for cover, Danny simply embraced the rain. Within two minutes he was soaked to the bone but finding the experience refreshing and energising, stayed out for a further thirty minutes. As he finally headed for the backdoor - *'all-time'* keepy-up record still intact - the rain had finally begun to relent. His sodden kit clung to his body as he grappled with adjusting the temperamental shower head. A minute later, he was standing under an equally welcome shower. This time, it warmed him to the bone and after a quick splash of shower gel, he was done. Danny quickly dressed before depositing his wet clothes in the laundry basket in the corner of his mum's room.

It was then that it caught his eye.

He wondered how he had he never spotted it before! Maybe because it wasn't especially eye-catching or interesting but all the same, Danny was intrigued by what was behind, or indeed, above it. A few moments later he'd placed the stepladders, retrieved from the garden, directly under the entrance. An entrance to a loft space. What harm could a quick look do? After all – when it came to exploring lofts, he was something of a specialist!

With being new to the house, travelling with few possessions and it being a rented property, neither Danny nor his mum had any need, or indeed business, in exploring the space. But this *'find'* had spiked his curiosity and he felt compelled to explore further despite the fact that he should have resisted the temptation.

The wooden entry panel was stuck fast but after a number of jolts from the base of Danny's right hand, he managed to shift the panel out of its frame. On hauling himself up into the loft he noticed two things.

Firstly, a handily-placed, string cord. When pulled downwards it enabled a solitary lightbulb to illuminate the immediate area. However, whereas the school loft was boarded, providing a number of walkways, this was very different. With just the joists and wooden beams below Danny's feet, they provided him with a very limited number of routes to explore the loft safely. Even so, he would just have to move carefully by placing one foot in front of the other, a little like a tightrope walker would move. Danny grabbed hold of the lightbulb itself, as it was still cool enough to do so. He turned it through ninety degrees to throw light further down the length of the loft space. As he glanced in the direction of the light, he was both surprised and confused in equal measure, by what he saw. This loft appeared to go on for ever and ever and in both directions. Danny soon realised this wasn't just his loft but the whole street's! Perplexed, he wondered who would design and build an *'open'* loft so that everybody would share the same enormous space. It was clear though, where the possessions of one house stopped and the neighbour's begun. The fact that Danny's neighbours were none other than the Doubty twins, made it all the more intriguing. He reminded himself that he was here to explore *'his'* belongings, even though *'his'* belongings were clearly the landlord's possessions or even a previous tenant's! There were no archaic log books or records to unearth here but there was plenty to rummage through and keep Danny busy, for a while at least. The fact that the loft benefited from an electricity supply and lightbulb made it relatively easy to root through the various boxes and objects. A pile of baby and toddler clothes, toys as well as books, weren't quite what Danny was hoping to find but it was at the bottom of this particular box that Danny found it – or touched it – at first.

A smooth, stretched, tight surface with what felt like wooden carvings around the sides. Digging deeper, Danny gained a more secure hold on the object and then tugged firmly and with both hands. The result was inevitable. The object began to work its way free from the base of the box and as Danny pulled it clear, he fell back sharply but safely against a vertical wooden beam, the object securely held in both hands.

It was quickly apparent to Danny that he was holding a drum, not especially big and one which could be placed on his lap and easily played. Whilst Danny wasn't particularly musical, he was instantly drawn towards this instrument but wasn't really able to appreciate why. However, he found he could immediately drum a simple beat with his fingers or the palm of his hand. This, coupled with the fact that Danny hardly owned any possessions, heightened his interest even further in this newly-found object. At that point he decided that for as long as he remained in this house, he would take *'personal care'* of the drum.

With his mind made up and drum in hand, he turned

the light off and stepped onto the top of the stepladder. He climbed back down into his mum's room, carefully placing the loft entrance panel back into its place. Danny's mum wasn't due home for a couple of hours, when her shift ended, so he had ample time to ensure everything was in place ahead of her return. He spent the time closely examining his find in the comfort of his own room. It wasn't just how it felt, which drew Danny towards it but also how it looked. He had seen drums before but nothing quite like this.

It was clearly ancient and Danny seriously considered if it was older than the house itself. He knew very little about drums but was aware that animal skins were often used for the head of drums. This appeared to be the case with this drum too. The majority of the drum was constructed from wood which had been skilfully fashioned into a goblet shape, with the top of the drum standing approximately sixty centimetres tall when the drum was placed on the floor. The drum head's circumference was of a similar size to that of a side plate and it was framed by black rope, no more than two centimetres in thickness. The same black rope then had as many as six additional strips of rope running vertically down the length of the goblet section of the drum. The drum's mid-section was its narrowest point before the circumference increased again towards the base of the drum. On closer inspection, Danny realised that the base was hollow and that the sound from the drum was stifled and much duller if it was placed on the floor and played. By holding the drum in the air, or better still by placing it between the knees at its narrowest point, Danny was able to appreciate the much richer and fulfilling sound the drum would then make when struck. In addition to the carving and situated at the foot of the drum, there was also a beautifully detailed pattern of coloured dots, which danced their way around the entire base. It provided a vibrant splash of colour to the drum and was about ten centimetres in height. The dominant colours were red, green and yellow but these were offset with splashes of white and blue too.

All in all, Danny was certain that the origin of this drum had to be marginally more exotic than Shropshire! Wherever it originated from, Danny felt like he had already made some sort of connection with this musical instrument.

With little focus on time, Danny was taken aback when he heard the front door go, signalling the return of his mother but he had already decided on his plan of action. Carefully making his way downstairs, he produced a steady beat from the drum with his right hand, whilst it was tucked under the crook of his left arm.

"Hi mum, what d'you make of my musical skills?" he asked with a grin.

"Hello you – where on earth did you get that from?" she replied, quizzically.

"Found it in the loft, you know, through that hatch in your bedroom?"

"Of course I know…" she hesitated, before continuing, "and you should know better than to explore somewhere you shouldn't!"

"Yeah, look mum, I'm sorry. I won't do it again but please can I keep this in my room? At least until we move house again, if we have to?"

Danny waited patiently for a reply before his mum finally answered his question.

"Only if you promise not to go up there again!"

"You got yourself a deal Mrs Bowen, now shake my hand," Danny added cheekily, before thrusting his hand towards his mother. She simply smiled, sighed then shook Danny firmly by the hand.

Danny was an absolute master at charming his mother whenever there was a need for it; she often thought it was all this practise that helped him to become a more confident person when out and about. So, even if it meant he often got his way, she figured it was a price worth paying. Little by little and certainly since moving to Shropshire, Danny's mum had witnessed his increasing confidence at first hand and it filled her with hope for the future. She was beginning to look forward, rather than always over her shoulder.

His new find also meant he was kept busy for the remainder of the holiday. It enabled her to get around the house and give it a good spring clean ahead of the landlord's visit to the house later that month.

As for Danny – he was simply obsessed with his drum. If he wasn't playing it, he found himself sketching it or simply holding it. Without prompting, he found himself writing a *'Fact File'* on the drum and in little more than a morning he had found out a great deal. He was pretty certain he had identified the type of drum thanks to an internet search. To Danny, his drum looked and sounded very much like a djembe drum and this find simply increased his natural curiosity in the object. It had looked exotic and beautiful on first inspection and now he knew this was the case. His detective work indicated it probably hailed from West Africa, most likely Mali. The djembe drum was indeed, a drum rich in history. Danny discovered that it had maybe been in use in Western Africa for a thousand years or more and that evening, he couldn't wait to share his news with his mum.

"So, to recap mum, the djembe drum has been around for at least thirty times longer than you and incredibly it is even more beautiful than you! It is still commonly used today in countries like Mali and the Ivory Coast and some call it the *'Talking Drum'* because... well, it sounds like the human voice and it is used to share important messages. Last but not least, mum – the skin of the drum probably used to belong to a goat!"

"Yuck..." she exclaimed, quickly handing the drum back to Danny, "but I am very impressed with your research and drumming skills, Danny," she replied, once Danny had paused to take a breath!

"Also, I reckon we should use it in assemblies too because the drum name comes from a saying which means, *'everyone gather together in peace'*. What d'you reckon mum, cool or what?" Danny continued.

"I'm incredibly impressed, my love," she replied whilst nodding in agreement.

Over the course of the weekend Danny's football sat next to the bins, neglected, his keepy-up record still intact. With his *'Fact File'* complete, he turned his attention to mastering the drum itself. The more he played it, the more he could relate to the analogy of the drum sounding like a human voice; Danny felt as if he could almost understand and communicate with the drum itself! By Sunday evening, he considered himself to be a skilled and accomplished drummer. Through a combination of research and practical drumming clips, courtesy of social media, he further developed his appreciation for this beautiful instrument. A growing awareness for the bass, slap and open tones of the drum, coupled with an ability to play it at increasing speed with both hands, meant that he was more than capable of composing various drumming pieces.

"So, the plan is to take your fact file and drum into school tomorrow, is it?" asked Danny's mum.

"Yep but actually I think I'll leave it until the Tuesday, mum. That way I get to practise for a few more hours after school tomorrow."

CHAPTER 3

The following morning, he woke with a spring in his step, enjoying both an early hours drumming session and the brighter mornings due to the clocks going back. His mood was still reasonably upbeat for this this time of year – a time of year when the summer was becoming a distant memory and winter was preparing to enter the fray.

On his brief journey to school that morning, Danny considered that there were very many reasons to be positive about life at present. Unsurprisingly, school was pretty much as it had been before half-term. It was a place where Danny felt safe and filled with an increasingly warm feeling that he actually belonged there too. He was bursting at the seams, desperate to tell Toby and Delilah of his exciting find over half-term but it would have to wait until the following day. *'Patience is a virtue!'*, whatever that means! His mum had delivered this wise saying, as he had jogged down the pathway to school that Monday morning.

Miss Patel somehow appeared to be filled with even more energy and positivity than she normally was, when Danny got into class. She went on to explain to the class that, thanks to their hard work ahead of half-term, a total of one hundred guests had now been identified and the next stage was to try and track the remaining ones down.

"In fact, there are two very special individuals but I'd like a few of you to turn detective and work out who I'm referring to. Lucy's table – you have this afternoon to look through the 'Log Books' and find the mystery duo. The only hints I will give you, is that you are looking for one of the school's first pupils. She then returned many years later, to work at the school. The second person is a grandfather to one of our younger teachers at Northernvale, who came to the school as a pupil!" Miss Patel stated, as she finished her explanation.

In the hall that lunchtime, Toby complained that it was 'unfair' that the challenge wasn't given to his table. "As long as we've got the answers by the end of school today, it really doesn't matter!" countered Delilah. Danny thought she was right – on both counts.

As it turned out, Lucy's table had come up with the goods by the end of school and were able to share their findings with the class. Firstly, a pupil called Florence Weston, was just four years old in 1919 and was present on the first day that Northenvale opened its doors. In 1959, the very same person returned to school as the new headmistress. For the next 'twenty-five years or so', Mrs Bailey (her married name) remained the headmistress, retiring in 1985. Miss Patel went on to explain that Mrs Bailey had long since passed away, back in the year 2000 but her daughter was still alive and lived just a couple of miles away in the next village.

It was then left to Joe to explain that the second individual was a Lawrence Anderson, who attended the school as a pupil in 1926. Well in his nineties and still alive, Joe explained that he was, in fact, the grandfather of Miss Williams, the school's KS1 teacher. Miss Williams had confirmed that he was now in a care home in Gloucestershire but would be keen to visit his old school maybe one more time.

"Well, there's only one thing for it, Miss," offered Lucy, "we need to invite that lady's daughter and Miss Williams's grandad as our most 'VIGers'!"

"Exactly, Lucy and what I love more and more about this every day, is that we keep finding connections between family and friends in our community that draw us closer and closer together," added Miss Patel, as the bell sounded to signal the end of school. As the children headed home, Danny doubled back on himself from the cloakroom into the classroom. He needed the green light for his plans for the next day.

"Oh, hi again, Danny," Miss Patel said, as she looked up from a pile of English books which she was marking.

"Hello again, Miss..." he hesitated before continuing, "I've found something special that I want to share with the class tomorrow, please? I know we don't do 'Show and Tell' in upper key stage 2 but could I do this... PLEASE?"

"Well, I'm certainly intrigued, Danny. Tell me more."

So Danny did so and in great detail.

After a ten-minute summary, Miss Patel delighted Danny by agreeing whole-heartedly to his request.

"It's wonderful that you've completed this over half-term and totally independently – I'd love to see if your drumming skills are at the level you suggest, see you tomorrow," Miss Patel continued, whilst indicating that the conversation was finished with and that Danny ought to head home.

After tea that evening, Danny did as he planned. He practised his 'Fact File' presentation and drumming session over and over again, including twice to his mum.

"It's great Danny but it's also ten o'clock and time for bed," his mum pointed out. It was a further hour before Danny fell asleep that evening but the next day arrived soon enough.

Once in school, the day dragged, reminding him of how slowly every day used to take at his previous schools. However, this time it was due to excitement and anticipation rather than boredom, anger or frustration.

"Class – finish the sentence you're on and then close your Science books. We need to finish a little earlier so as to enjoy *'Danny's Show'!"* she added, before she smiled in his direction.

"Huh... Danny's *'Show-Off'* Show," more like, added Millie unpleasantly, under her breath but just loud enough for Danny to hear. In the past, this type of comment would have enraged Danny and there would have been a response, most likely physical. However, that was then and this was now. By not responding, he knew his non-reaction was the last thing Millie was hoping for.

"Danny's Show!" repeated Toby, whilst gently ribbing his pal. "You've kept this quiet – I can't wait," he offered by way of encouragement towards his friend.

"Patience is a virtue," replied Danny, grinning. He now knew the meaning of this phrase and thought he'd used it with some aplomb!

"Ay, you what?" was the only response that Toby could muster.

Danny started with his interactive IT presentation, explaining how he found the drum at home – but neglected to mention that he'd clambered up into the loft – before sharing his 'Fact File' in detail, as well as the history of the djembe drum. Throughout this entire period, Danny glanced around the class on three, possibly four occasions and was relieved to see that his classmates were hanging on his every word. Even the Doubty twins resisted the temptation to make any further unwelcome remarks. It had gone just as Danny had rehearsed. On its conclusion he was encouraged by a very generous round of applause and even a few cheers.

Growing in confidence, Danny announced, "Now, who wants to hear this wonderful instrument, played live, by yours truly?"

Further cheering provided that last piece of confidence Danny needed. Outwardly, he was calm, collected and confident and at ease with the drum: inwardly, he felt the first flutters of nerves, deep from within but spreading upwards at an alarming rate. Trying his best to fight this unwelcome emotion - he simply picked up the drum, clasped it between his knees and tilted the drum head slightly towards himself, just as he knew he should do.

As he began to play with a steady bass tone, he felt those last-minute nerves melt away, along with any lingering awkwardness.

This was it.

He was at one with the drum and was hardly able to contain the positive energy coursing through his body. His smile was beaming and natural, his audience engrossed, as was his class teacher.

The pitch, the pace and the feel of the drum were just perfect. He played with skill, accuracy and freedom, just as he had hoped. Two minutes later he was able to exhale loudly, place the drum down and provide all with a deep, elegant bow.

He wasn't though ready for what happened next. Miss Patel stood and applauded with such enthusiasm. Within moments, the whole class followed her lead and Danny was simply overwhelmed. As the applause subsided, Miss Patel gave Danny a hug stating that he was *'an absolute star'*.

With Danny still on a high, he took the opportunity to explain the intricate nature of the drum, including the bass, slap and open tones you could play on it. Inevitably, everybody seemed to want to try their hand at playing the djembe. Therefore, it was agreed that he would keep the drum in school for the next week so that the entire class could each have a go playing it.

"So, how did it go Danny?" asked his mum impatiently, as she stepped through the front door later that afternoon.

"Just the best, mum, Miss Patel even hugged me at the end of it!"

"Oh, well done, my love. I'm just so proud…" she began before her voice trailed off, leading to Danny receiving his second big hug in a matter of minutes.

That evening, Danny's mum received a message from school, stating how impressed they were with his exploits and that they were intending on awarding him a certificate in assembly, as long as he played the drum in front of the whole school. This was the icing on the cake for Danny and that Friday, he stole the show – again! It provided the perfect end to the best school week that Danny could ever remember, let alone imagine.

The following week started with a miserable, wet Monday but a very unexpected conversation. During that morning's wet break, Mrs Richards – the school secretary of many years – asked to speak to Danny. Being summoned by Mrs Richards was a very rare event, rumour had it that she didn't especially like children and most definitely preferred her pet dogs! Reputation enough, to make Danny feel slightly nervous as he approached the office door.

Unbeknown to Danny she had snuck into the hall, through the back door, the previous Friday to listen to Danny's drumming.

As he tentatively knocked, Mrs Richards beckoned him to open the door, which he did.

"Now Danny," started Mrs Richards, choosing to do away with any niceties, "I know that the children and probably some staff, think that I have been here for a hundred years, never mind the school, but whilst it's not that long, it has been many years. The reason I'm telling you this is because it's linked to your drumming last Friday," continued Mrs Richards.

"Oh right, okay…" replied Danny, who understandably had absolutely no idea in which direction this conversation was going but felt the need to say something.

"Anyhow," she continued, "I am as certain as I am sat here that the school actually possess a set of djembe drums, from goodness knows how many years ago! Certainly much longer compared to my twenty years. I can recall a retired former teacher talking about the drums in the loft from many moons ago. And I can't imagine they've gone very far in the last half century or so!" she smiled. "What I'm saying to you Danny, is why not ask Miss Patel to retrieve them, so then your whole class can drum together? The only place they could possibly have been stored would be the school loft and you're an expert at climbing into our school loft, aren't you?"

Finding his voice again, Danny asked if Miss Patel knew of this.

"Well, Miss Patel has only been here for two years, so I very much doubt it," replied Mrs Richards, before her attention was diverted to a ringing phone on her desk.

A quick smile and thumbs up from the school secretary signalled the end of the conversation. Danny turned on his heels and headed quickly back to class.

"So that's what Mrs Richards wanted to talk to me about, Miss. We've probably got a full set of djembe drums in the loft. Can you believe it?" he asked his teacher rhetorically. "So, can we get them down, please?"

"I'm not sure, Danny," came the underwhelming response from Miss Patel, "look, it can't be any time soon and we aren't absolutely certain we have them but leave it with me. I will speak to Mr Stanley and get back to you."

Danny was keen to share the news with his classmates, which he inevitably did do. He figured he might need additional support to persuade Miss Patel. However, this didn't speed up the decision-making process. Danny couldn't understand why Miss Patel wouldn't look to retrieve the drums as soon as possible. He had learnt over time, that teachers were an unpredictable bunch and accepted that he may need to play the *long game* and wait patiently for a decision.

As a result, the autumn term slowly meandered towards its conclusion. Danny had been able to keep his djembe drum in school and gave up every dinner time to provide one-to-one tutorials on how to play the drum for his classmates. This had included both Doubty twins but thankfully not at the same time! Neither of these were the most comfortable sessions but he felt he ought to be fair to all. He did though remind them of the Halloween tripping incident and quietly warned each of them not to make a similar mistake again. In truth, relations with the duo had been thawing of late, especially as Danny's mum seemed to be getting on very well with the Doubty twins' mother – not an especially welcome development from Danny's point of view but he figured it couldn't be helped.

As ever, Christmas 'arrived' in mid-November at Northernvale Primary, leaving Danny to wonder if it was like that at every primary school.

It was though reassuring that Miss Patel took the time to have a couple of conversations with Danny, reinforcing that she'd not forgotten about his request.

The temperature took a real tumble over the course of late-November into December, with winter slowly but surely taking a strangle-hold on the school. The ageing school boilers responded by grumbling and gurgling away all day trying to keep the chilliest of the conditions at arm's length. To Danny though, this winter seemed less barren and not as harsh as previous ones. There was no doubt he was drawing increasing natural warmth from the school community and his school friendships.

He found himself studiously learning the words for the Carol Service off by heart and sung them with enthusiasm; he helped out with props and staging for the nativity play and even returned happily for the evening performance too.

The class's Christmas-related highlight had to be the visit to the old folks' home to share carols and conversations. The class possessed a naturally keen interest in the older generation, after their research work earlier that term. This was heightened further when Miss Patel took the opportunity to introduce two specific residents to Wrekin Class. The two of them – Harold Beaumont and Dot Morrow – were former pupils of the school, again both in their nineties and both with an invitation as two of the school's one hundred special guests.

"I hope they're up for a party in July, Danny!" whispered Toby.

"Yeah, they don't look primed to go at the moment but I reckon they'll get plenty of rest before July, so that they're ready for the big day!" replied his friend.

As the last day of term came and went, Danny headed home with a strong feeling of déjà vu. He was full of positivity, just as he was when finishing for the October half-term but this felt even more satisfying and nourishing to Danny. He was settled in his new home, with a new environment and new friends and it was very rare of late, that Danny would find himself casting his mind back to life before his move to Shropshire.

It also dawned on Danny that his fear of his father had simply evaporated. That man, full of anger, aggression and rage would not and could not reappear – not when Danny and his mum were happier than he could ever remember. It simply wouldn't be fair. In fact, Danny would be happy for his mum to have a new partner and happy that he would most likely never see his father again.

It had been as an eight-year-old and nearly three years ago that Danny last lived permanently in the same house as his dad. There were a handful of very vague but happy memories when he was extremely young but the overriding emotion was one of fear. Danny had never been hurt by his father, not physically anyhow but he now understood the emotional distress his father had caused him by the levels of cruelty and aggression he had routinely displayed towards Danny's mother.

It was one particular night, a little less than eighteen months previously, that Danny could recall most vividly. Crashing, shouting, banging and his mother's tears as the police had arrived late at night, arresting Danny's father. Danny had felt so alone, cowering under his duvet until the police left but when reunited with his mum, he promised to protect her from that point on and felt that he'd delivered on his pledge.

Social services had helped, listened and supported Danny at home and in school. They had, most importantly, found the house which Danny now considered his home. He had never mentioned his father to his best friends, only to say that he didn't see him anymore. They had sensed, simply by the hurried nature of Danny's arrival in their lives, that life wasn't straightforward for him and had therefore never pried or asked awkward questions. He had always appreciated this.

So, of course, once Christmas arrived it was, for the fourth time in a row, a 'Christmas for Two'.

Opportunities to meet up with school friends were restricted in the following two weeks, due to the cold, short days and those same friends visiting family, far and wide.

However, a sleepover at Toby's proved popular for two reasons. Firstly, he was allowed to stay up beyond midnight, owing to it being New Year's Eve and secondly, his mum was invited too! The ideal way to see in a new year which he hoped and wished would be just half as good as the previous six months.

CHAPTER 4

Danny's positivity was rewarded on the first day back! It was the arrival of Mr Stanley in Wrekin Class, sporting a smile, which aroused suspicions amongst the pupils.

"Mr Stanley and I have been chatting for a few weeks now and we have a proposal for you!" Miss Patel said as she addressed the whole class.

"And in addition to this and before Miss Patel lets the cat out of the bag, we will need focus, determination and teamwork from every one of you..." continued Mr Stanley, "because we are prepared to put aside two hours, yes TWO HOURS or more of your weekly timetable, between now and July!"

Both Miss Patel and Mr Stanley then expanded on their plan for the class. Not only had they agreed to hopefully locate and retrieve the drums from the loft, the class were also to open the *'Centenary Celebration Day'* with a carnival-type parade of all pupils, around the village. Mr Stanley had spoken to a former member of staff who was pretty certain the drums would be *'up there somewhere'*, in the loft. Drums successfully located, Wrekin Class would then lead this procession with their instruments and share the message - spreading centenary celebrations to all within their community. Mr Stanley was even going to contact the Highways Agency and council to request special road closures to make the route safe for the very youngest and oldest to take part in. To top it off, Danny was to lead this colourful, noisy procession. He was, after all, the *'Master Drummer'* as Mr Stanley had referred to him.

This was a huge amount for Wrekin Class to take in and at morning break there was only one topic of conversation.

"It's going to be unbelievable, Danny and you get to lead the procession. You'll be brilliant!" gushed Delilah. Danny felt one hundred feet tall and all of this, thanks to a chance finding of a neglected, long-forgotten drum!

"Even the Doubty twins are excited, Danny – did you see their faces?" continued Delilah.

"But…" Danny found himself pausing and mumbling as doubt began to penetrate his thoughts, "what if I mess it up?" he eventually asked.

With a grin and a simple statement, Toby quelled his fears.

"You're Danny Bowen. And Danny Bowen doesn't do *'mess-ups'*!"

That evening, Danny explained the idea to his mum, including the fact that once they'd located all of the djembe drums, he and Miss Patel would be responsible for teaching the class to play the drum like he did and then deliver the goods on the 1st July.

"Is that all?" she asked, whilst laughing.

"You play that drum like a natural, like it's almost attached to you… part of you. You'll be wonderful. What's not to like about the proposal?" she added.

Danny headed to bed with a warm glow that evening, finding it hard to get to sleep.

On awakening the next morning and with the exciting proposal having now fully sunk in, he couldn't wait to get into school to tell everyone that he was up for the challenge. Miss Patel was able to confirm that Mr Stanley was to go on his *'drum hunt'* on the Friday of that week and to Danny's delight, he was to be allowed out of class to help locate the drums.

That Friday afternoon came soon enough and after placing the caretaker's stepladders below the loft entry, Mr

Stanley headed to Wrekin Class to collect Danny.

"Right Danny, you know this loft as well as I do, since you were up here as recently as I was!"

"Yeah, I was and actually I'm becoming a bit of a specialist in entering lofts. But this could be a bit like looking for a needle in a haystack," Danny exaggerated.

"Not a problem for us Danny," replied Mr Stanley, "we'll need to get our hands dirty as they're certainly not stored in plain sight. It'll need us to shift a few of those dust sheets around to locate them and it's not especially bright up there either."

At this point Mr Stanley smiled and handed Danny a large torch, whilst picking up his own.

"We come prepared; let's do this Danny!" added Mr Stanley in a theatrical voice before stepping onto the lower rungs of the stepladder. As Mr Stanley hoisted himself up into the loft, Danny followed quickly behind.

"Steady Danny!" came the voice of Mrs Richards from below as he climbed off the top of the ladder. She had arrived in the nick of time, so as to foot the ladder whilst Danny hauled himself up into the loft space. Mr Stanley was already stood, hands on hips, surveying the scene, as Danny got to his feet. Following closely behind were the head and shoulders of Mrs Richards along with a suggestion that she would remain there until the drums had been successfully located.

Danny headed to the area in which they'd unearthed the school records earlier in the school year. Mr Stanley headed off in the opposite direction. Ten minutes into the initial search and neither had enjoyed any success. Mrs Richards's calmness was being tested to the limit, leading to her suggesting she join in the hunt.

"No need Mrs Richards, who's there to answer the phone if it rings or if a visitor needs signing in?"

"Good point, Mr Stanley. My mum is always telling me patience is a virtue," Danny added, mischievously.

Mrs Richards shook her head, raising an eyebrow in Danny's direction and simply suggested that the pair ought to pull their fingers out and find the drums. Danny felt a degree of frustration too, surely they had to be here somewhere? It was a further fifteen minutes later and having both swapped to the opposite and final two corners of the loft, that they struck gold.

Danny had scrambled under a low roof joist and it was the second large dust sheet, shrouding an area the size of a large dining table, which he had peeled back to discover a sight for sore eyes.

An array of dusty, djembe drums, half of them the size of his drum and the other half much larger versions of the same drum. His heart skipped a beat as his smile lit up the darkest corner of that school loft.

Mission accomplished.

"Get in there!" he shouted gaining Mrs Richards's attention from the office, let alone Mr Stanley's.

"Wonderful, that looks the ticket!" exclaimed Mr Stanley as he stooped over to where Danny was crouched, before patting him firmly on the back.

"I'll tell Miss Patel and the class," came the voice from the excited head and shoulders of Mrs Richards, before she descended back down the stepladder.

It was a call for action stations in Wrekin Class. It was decided that what was needed, to remove this bounty from the loft, was a human chain. Miss Patel had more volunteers then she knew what to do with, before settling on just six. The plan was a simple one. Mr Stanley would collect each of the drums one at a time, walk across the beams and hand the drum to Danny, who would be positioned at the top of the stepladder, replacing Mrs Richards. From there, Danny would carefully pass the drum onto a classmate, positioned two rungs down from him and so on. The last two pupils in the chain would then carry each drum into the school library, where an area had been cleared for their temporary storage.

By now, the djembe drum find had spread like wild fire, in the main due to Mrs Richards informing each and every class. She did enjoy being the bearer of exciting news.

Mr Stanley's role was the trickiest. He had to stoop low, under the roof joists, to pick up each drum, before bending down again to pass the drum to Danny. Danny was though, a little dismayed to find Millie directly below him on the stepladder but at least she had been less of a hindrance more recently.

Danny worked out that he would then have to twist his upper body between receiving the drum from Mr Stanley, above, and passing it to Millie, below. Once the process of removing the drums began, Danny started to count them, one by one, needing a grand total of thirty-two to ensure everybody had a drum, including Miss Patel. The smaller drums totalled eighteen – an encouraging start but the larger drums presented an added difficulty.

The diameter of the drum head was much larger and almost the dimensions of the loft entrance itself. However, Mr Stanley soon calculated that the larger drums could be safely delivered if each drum was slightly tilted when delivered to Danny. In no time at all the job was almost done. Danny had already counted thirty-five, which he was more than satisfied with. With one solitary drum left, it was then that a spanner was thrown into the works.

"Last drum on its way, Danny!" shouted Mr Stanley, triumphantly, as he crouched below the beams for the final time. As Danny looked on, it appeared as if time itself froze! A split-second later, Danny heard a shriek of pain, followed by a mumbled rant from his headteacher.

"You OK, Mr Stanley?" enquired a bemused Danny.

"Err, yes and no, Danny!" came the reply before he continued, "well I've got my hands on the last drum, as you may be able to see but I can't actually move!"

"Oh!" was the only response Danny could muster, before adding, "but can't you just stand up slowly and walk over to me with that last drum, like you've done with the other thirty-five?"

"I'd like nothing more," came the reply, "but I can't move a muscle. My back's gone. Frozen! I'm stuck Danny – it must be all this stooping and bending," came the pained reply.

"MISS... MISS!" shouted the panicked Danny, from the top of the ladder.

"MR STANLEY'S STUCK IN THE LOFT. HE THINKS HIS BACK'S GONE!"

A few stifled giggles came from Millie and her classmates, further down the ladder and in the corridor, where Miss Patel was now standing.

"Oh dear!" Miss Patel eventually contributed, just as unhelpfully.

There was nothing else for it, in times of crisis, Mrs Richards would know what to do, so Lucy was sent to collect her, without delay.

"Well, what do you expect *me* to do about this?" announced Mrs Richards, as she turned the corner. In truth, there was little that anybody could do. Simply put, the headteacher was stuck in the loft, doubled-over and totally incapable of putting one foot in front of the other. After a short period of silence, Mrs Richards sent everybody packing, including Miss Patel, back to class.

"Hang on Danny, you stay with me and keep an eye on our headteacher."

So, Danny remained at the top of the ladder, peering into the darkness, where the solitary figure could be seen, motionless, resting both palms of his hands on the drum head to relieve himself from the intense discomfort. Danny felt the need to make conversation but was unsure what to say.

"Bet you didn't expect to find yourself in this position when you turned up for work today, Mr Stanley?"

"Hmm, you're not wrong there, Danny," came the curt response.

"I could always come up and get that last drum, if that…" Danny's offer of help was abruptly interrupted by the returning Mrs Richards.

"No, I don't think so Danny but you can pass these up to Mr Stanley," she added, before handing him a glass of water and two tablets. Danny duly placed the items next to the loft entrance, on one of the wooden beams.

Mrs Richards shouted loudly and from below, "Mr Stanley, you'll simply need to take these painkillers and wait for them to take effect. There's nothing else for it."

"But I can't even stand up straight, let alone walk!" he replied.

"Miss, why don't I climb up? I can put the tablets and water on the drum for Mr Stanley," Danny offered.

"That makes sense Danny. I can't move from here and this loft isn't especially warm. Please bring them over to me."

With Mrs Richards continuing to foot the ladder, Danny did as instructed.

"There you go Mr Stanley, I'll just put them on the drum if that's OK?"

"Thanks, Danny," replied the stationary figure.

As Danny retreated back down the ladder, he was sent off to class by Mrs Richards but she did ask that he pop his head back in the loft every fifteen minutes or so, just to check his headteacher was OK and hopefully slightly more mobile.

For the next thirty minutes, Danny became the messenger

for Wrekin Class, paying two visits to the school's prone headteacher, on each occasion glancing briefly into the loft before returning immediately to class. On arriving for his third visit, with his headteacher very much in the same predicament, Danny paused for a moment, feeling as though he really ought to offer at least a few words of encouragement.

"It feels a bit chilly up here, Mr Stanley. D'you want me to get a coat or jumper or somethin' from Mrs Richards?" he asked.

"Oh, hi Danny. Didn't see you pop up there," he smiled, "I'm absolutely fine to be honest. Back's barely any better but don't worry, there's no danger of hyperthermia setting in, so no need for the extra layers!"

"Right, okay… well I'll come back in another fifteen minutes then," replied Danny as he began to climb down the rungs of the stepladder.

"Hang on a second, Danny!" came the call from the loft. Danny climbed back up into sight.

"Yes, Mr Stanley?" he asked expectantly.

"You've been a pupil at this school for over six months now, Danny. Tell me, what's made the difference compared to your old schools?" asked Danny's headteacher.

"What d'you mean Sir?" replied Danny, slightly confused.

"Sorry, Danny," Mr Stanley responded, "I could have phrased that a little better. What I meant to say is, your attitude towards school and your behaviour has been wonderful at Northernvale. When I received the paperwork from your previous schools, I didn't expect you to settle in anywhere near as well as you have done. I thought you might struggle, to be honest with you. I also thought you would certainly struggle to avoid conflict and make the right decisions, Danny. It's wonderful… what you've done. I was just asking you why you think it's gone so well," Mr Stanley clarified.

"Oh right, I get it. That's easy Mr Stanley. You helped.

When I met you, you wanted to get to know me and you didn't judge me. And then you introduced me to Miss Patel. She's amazing, Mr Stanley."

"In what way, Danny?" the intrigued headteacher asked.

Danny reminded Mr Stanley of that first visit to school the previous June and how Miss Patel took thirty minutes out of the classroom to chat with him and put his mind at rest. He explained that no other teacher had ever done that, no other teacher had even listened as carefully as Miss Patel had, on that day.

"I'll never forget that Mr Stanley and I never want to let Miss down. My teacher before Miss Patel told me that I had better learn to control my temper, or I'd be out and he also told me that there wasn't even enough room in the classroom for me. He said that the class was full already and that there wasn't even a chair for me. I didn't belong at that school and when I was excluded, I didn't even care, Mr Stanley! I belong in this school and I've never felt like that before," Danny continued, wondering whether he had said too much.

"That's nice of you to speak of Miss Patel like that and I understand what you're saying, Danny. However, everybody is entitled to a second chance. A fresh start, especially school children. And you've well and truly taken your opportunity in this school and it's difficult to imagine Northernvale without you! What we love about you is your positivity. It's infectious and by that, I mean in a good way, Danny. Your teacher, and the school staff, have a lot of time for you. Although I can't help regretting agreeing to you starting at Northernvale..." Mr Stanley added, before smiling and saying, "because if you'd gone to a different school, I'd be in my warm office right now, rather than stuck in a freezing loft and unable to move - on the very verge of hypothermia and death, no doubt!" laughed Mr Stanley, through the pain.

Danny laughed too before thanking his headteacher and dipping out of sight.

The end of the school day was rapidly approaching, with just fifteen minutes until the bell, when Danny made his fourth and final visit to the loft. Mr Stanley was sitting on the drum, slightly dejected and clearly still in pain, waiting for the painkillers to take effect. Danny thought better than to suggest that Mr Stanley could cause some damage to the drum, seeing as he was perched on top of it. In fairness, everything was as expected but Danny, nor Mr Stanley, could not possibly have been prepared for what happened next.

As Danny peered across at Mr Stanley, the headteacher seemed calmer, somehow less frustrated, even though he was now one hour on from becoming stranded in the chilly loft. Danny chose not to ask how his back was, for the umpteenth time that afternoon. Instead, he felt compelled to turn away from Mr Stanley and look into the far corner of the loft space. At precisely the same time, Mr Stanley seemed to experience exactly the same urge - to turn and focus on the same corner.

The reason for this was simple but extraordinary too – there was movement. Not a scurrying or scampering you might expect in a loft, possibly created by a small rodent, such as a mouse, seeking cover.

This was different. It couldn't be any more different.

The movement was calm and it felt purposeful. Danny, along with his headteacher, were now both transfixed, even though there appeared nothing to be transfixed by! Danny opened his mouth to speak but, in the same moment, felt the need to say nothing at all.

It, whatever *'it'* was, slowly but surely began to take a form. A non-descript, grainy blur gradually grew in size, initially from no bigger than the size of a fist. It was very obvious to both that it was slowly increasing in size but was also mesmeric in its form and impossible to divert their attention away from.

Danny felt overwhelmed but intrigued too. There was no hint of fear or panic in his body language, nor that of Mr Stanley. As Danny began to make sense of this vision, it took his breath away.

There were no longer two of them in the loft.

There were *three*.

A serene, middle-aged lady was simply staring back at them. She was calm and unmoved. Danny detected what looked like a faint trace of a smile on her face. Trying to make sense of this, logic quickly told him there were only two possible explanations. He figured that his mind was either playing tricks on him or he was witnessing what could only be described as a paranormal experience!

At this point both Danny and Mr Stanley slowly turned and looked at each other. No words were exchanged, but that look between them, confirmed to the pair that they were both witnessing the same event unfold.

Again, they both refocused on the lady in the corner. It was most definitely a smile on her face, that much was clearer to Danny now. This hypnotic figure was wearing old-fashioned clothing but not from the Victorian Era. Danny thought that a typical ghost – if such a thing could exist – might often be adorned in Victorian clothing. No, this was different.

Old fashioned but positively modern, compared to that period of history. Her clothes were worn but still surprisingly colourful, the jumper she wore was patterned and so was her skirt. It was long and flowing, almost down to her ankles. He hair was neat and short towards the back but on the top of her head, it was almost a crimped, curly style.

There was something else too.

Danny noticed her unusual posture, she wasn't standing at all but appeared to exactly mirror Mr Stanley. He was still sitting on that final drum, hunched forward with his right hand on the small of his back.

Whilst the female figure had no drum, she too was *'sitting'* identically to how he was, right arm placed on the small of her back.

What happened next really did frighten Danny for the first time, but he felt incapable of any sort of movement, as if paralysed. The figure began to interact with Mr Stanley – Danny now felt disconnected as her gaze was firmly fixed on the headteacher and not him. He was quickly learning that witnessing what appeared to be a ghost was one thing but seeing it interact - was something else altogether!

Very slowly, she raised her right index finger to her lips and made a shushing shape with her lips, although Danny could hear no sound and wondered why this lady would request silence when you could hear a pin drop anyway. She was focused intently on Mr Stanley at this point but Danny continued to watch, open-mouthed in sheer amazement.

She moved from her *'seated'* position to one of standing. It was a careful, deliberate movement and at no point whilst standing upright did she take her eyes off Mr Stanley. She was attempting to communicate with him. The figure stood bolt upright, approximately ten metres from Mr Stanley, who was still sitting the other side of the loft, on the drum. Danny's head and shoulders, at least, remained positioned at the loft entrance directly between the two of them.

However, it was now Danny that the old lady headed towards. Again, very deliberately and very slowly. The incredibly calm atmosphere did not change, although the chill in the air was now far more evident to him. Despite this, Danny felt no urge to dip below the loft entrance and race down the stepladder. The figure was now solely focused on the entrance to such an extent that Danny wondered if the lady could even see him, or indeed if she now had any interest in him.

When she came to a halt, that long, flowing dress no more than thirty centimetres from Danny, he took just one, almost involuntary step back from the top of the stepladder. Again, she looked over at Mr Stanley and smiled before bending down, as if to climb onto the top of the stepladder herself. However, as she did this, she simply faded away, back to that grainy blur and then nothing!

Danny stepped back up the stepladder, just in time to witness Mr Stanley stand up, with no difficulty or awkwardness, gather up the drum and effortlessly walk to the loft entrance.

"She's shown you what to do... she's shown you what to do..." Danny mumbled to nobody in particular, as he stepped down each rung of the stepladder, before footing it for Mr Stanley. Moments later, they were standing alongside each other - that last drum placed down between them - back in the corridor. As they looked at each other, any possible exchange of words was cut short by the shrill ring of the school bell. Almost instantly, the corridor was transformed into a heaving, thronging mass, as children busied themselves with their own end-of-day arrangements.

"It's home time, Danny. I'll see you tomorrow," said Mr Stanley in a monotone voice before simply walking off in the direction of his office. No opportunity was given for Danny to respond to Mr Stanley's statement. So, he simply gathered up that last drum and placed it in the library. He then collected his coat and bag and headed off home, without delay.

CHAPTER 5

That evening, as Danny prepared for bed, he knew he'd get little or no sleep. Adrenalin still racing through his system – he tried to make sense of what had unfolded earlier that day in school. He had been uncharacteristically quiet at the dinner table that evening, picking and playing with his sausage and mash rather than eating it. He had made the decision that it was best to say absolutely nothing, mainly due to fearing what others might think of him.

It was at some point after three o'clock in the morning that Danny did fall asleep but it wasn't a deep sleep, more of a fitful one, leading to him waking very tired the following morning.

"Danny, you can't go to school without any breakfast at all! How many times have I told you that breakfast is the most important meal of the day?" Danny's mum continued.

"I've had some juice, mum – I don't want anything else, thanks," he replied wearily.

On his way to school, he decided he would wait for Mr Stanley to talk to him first, rather than the other way around. Danny spent the morning on 'auto-pilot' detached from the class, simply waiting. He counted three occasions when Mr Stanley could easily have spoken to him, without drawing attention to any conversation they might have – but nothing. His headteacher was just as he always was and the only exchange they had came right at the end of the school day. Mr Stanley had seen the class off and simply asked Danny if he had had a good day. Nothing more and no suggestion he wanted much of a response from Danny. Also, a cloakroom full of children was a peculiar choice too - Danny was hardly likely to suggest he'd been preoccupied with the ghost they'd both seen previously! It was as if Mr Stanley was pretending it hadn't even happened.

As that school week passed, the same pattern was played out. There was no conversation between the two, other than pleasantries. Danny began to refocus on his friends and school, he slept better too, figuring that seeing there was little or no fear connected to the episode at the start of the week, maybe he shouldn't worry too much about it – very much like his headteacher was clearly doing.

Danny had also wondered who the ghostly figure was and why she had clearly wanted to help Mr Stanley. After all, he considered that there was usually meant to be a reason behind a ghostly apparition. So, what was that reason and did she want or need Danny's help?

Over the course of the next week, things retuned to a form of normality for Danny. School continued to go well and he continued to work hard – a point mentioned by Miss Patel at the spring term parents' evening.

In addition, a steady flow of responses continued to wing their way into school, meaning that Wrekin Class's 100 'VI-Gers' target crept closer and closer. Danny continued to deliver his drumming sessions and was now completing extra sessions with five or six of his peers at a time. Before long, he found that he wasn't being drawn back to the events of that last visit to the school loft.

At home though, his attention was being drawn elsewhere. He couldn't help but notice that his mother and Mrs Doubty were getting on better than ever. Whilst he wasn't quite so irritated by the twins of late, he still found this blossoming relationship unsettling. After tea, one evening, he decided to take matters into his own hands.

"Mum, can I ask you a question? Just one?"

"Of course you can, Danny… you don't normally ask me if you can ask a question but ask away," she replied.

"How come you're best mates with the twins' mum now? You've been over there loads in the last week and then today, I get back from school and she's in our kitchen!" finished Danny, hoping that his mum wouldn't be too defensive when answering the question.

"Well…" she started in reply, pausing to give herself some thinking time, "we've got more in common than I thought."

Danny screwed his face up by way of a response before exclaiming, "We've got *nothing* in common with that lot!"

He was unable to hide the disgust in his voice.

"What I mean is, Rebecca and I have things in common," she added.

"No, you haven't, mum! We live on the same street as them and that's about all we have in common!" interrupted Danny before he stood up, marched angrily out of the kitchen and stomped up the stairs to his room.

An uneasy silence descended on the house for the next half hour, until Danny's mum headed upstairs, armed with a chocolate-chip cookie, by way of a peace-offering. She knocked the door gently, turning the handle and entering before being invited in.

"Can I explain, Danny… please?"

Reluctantly, Danny shuffled across to one side of his bed, offering her the vacant half in which to sit but he said nothing. He was keen to reinforce the fact that he wasn't happy about the whole situation. After carefully placing the plate, on which the cookie sat, on his bedside cabinet, she began her explanation. Danny listened, resisting the temptation to interrupt his mother. As she presented things from her perspective, Danny felt his mood soften as her explanation enabled him to better understand things from her point of view. There was no disputing that both mothers had to single-handedly bring up their respective children in the absence of a partner. That was a similarity which hadn't previously crossed Danny's mind.

Despite the issues between Danny and the twins, his mum was able to explain that both she and Rebecca were good company for each other and Danny also knew that his mother did sometimes feel lonely and that other adult company might not be such a bad thing.

"OK, mum... but don't ever consider inviting Mille and Mattie over here for tea!"

Whilst both smiling, his mum promised him that she would do no such thing.

The following day in school, Miss Patel was able to confirm that the school office had now heard from all of those who had been invited to the centenary celebrations and that the one hundred VIGers target had, indeed, been achieved. This news was greeted by an almighty cheer in Wrekin Class. To add to the excited mood in class, there was another intriguing development with the arrival of a letter, for the attention of the class. Miss Patel explained that one of the most important guests of all – the daughter of one of the first pupils and former headmistress – was able to visit the class in early June.

"We found out her identity, Miss," interrupted Lucy, "so can you read out the letter, please?"

"OK, Lucy. Listen carefully, then," replied Miss Patel.

Dear Wrekin Class,
Thank you for taking the time to write to me recently. I can confirm that you're absolutely spot on with your research. My mother was a pupil in the school in 1919 and also returned as the headmistress some forty years later in 1959. Such a long time ago! I can remember your beautiful school

but sadly I never attended it myself. I was fifteen when my mother became the headmistress but I do recall visiting the school, often with my mother during the school holidays.

It's got to be more than fifty or sixty years since I last visited, so I would be honoured and delighted to attend on the 1st July, later this year. In fact, Miss Patel has invited me to talk to your class about my family memories of the school in early June, which I'd be delighted to do. I think I'll be your proudest guest on the 1st July, when I attend on behalf of my mother. I can't wait to see you all later this school year.

All my love,
Diane Bailey

"That sounds great Miss. I can't wait to meet her," added Lucy, enthusiastically.

On the Friday of that week, Miss Patel read the letter out in *'Awards Assembly'*, so that everybody in the school was aware of the planned visit.

The following weekend witnessed snowfall which lasted for thirty-six hours. It was on a scale Danny had never seen before. By late Sunday evening he was able to wade out knee-deep in fresh, crisp snow. His mum left the kitchen light on so that he and Delilah could build their army of snowmen before snowballing the back of the house, ahead of taking aim at each other.

Whilst there was no more snowfall that evening, the freezing conditions ensured little changed. On arriving in the school playground the following morning, Danny was delighted to see more untouched snow than he knew what to do with. Mr Stanley used his assembly to remind the pupils how to play safely in the snow and even designated half of the playground for KS2 pupils to hold a snowball fight.

As the children raced out, later that morning, wellies, hats, gloves and scarves donned, the fun could begin. To add to the excitement, Mr Stanley, Mr Fowler and Miss Williams happily joined in the snowball fight. Danny noted with interest that Miss Patel was absent, questioning her bravery but content with three legitimate *'teacher targets',* Danny decided to take the matter up with his class teacher later on that morning.

"This looks like a very foolish decision; this was your idea wasn't it Mr Fowler?" hollered Mr Stanley as all three staff ducked and dived as if their lives depended upon it. Of course, it was a futile battle – more than sixty children versus three was only ever going to end in one way. Total carnage!

"Ceasefire... ceasefire," shouted Miss Williams as all three headed for the refuge of the staff room. Of course, the fun continued during lunchtime and despite no further snow falling, there was still more than enough sitting on the playground surface.

"That'll do me," panted Toby, as he raced away from the snowballing zone to relative sanctuary.

"My hands are freezing and I've lost a glove somewhere – it's too cold to go on," he added.

In truth, Danny didn't mind the break either; sitting down heavily on the bench next to his best mate.

"I can't believe how stupid Mr Stanley and the teachers were at breaktime!" laughed Danny.

"Yeah, Mr Fowler took at least six direct hits to the face. It was class!" agreed Toby.

Conversation between the two trailed off before their attention was drawn towards Mattie Doubty, who came hurtling out of the snowballing zone, cradling the most enormous snowball in the palm of his right hand. Both boys instantly knew what he was going to do but neither could move quick enough to take preventative measures!

As Mattie raced past the seated duo – no more than a blur – he unleashed the giant snowball with great velocity from point-blank range. The snowball made painful contact with Toby's face, exploding dramatically on impact. A tearful Toby collapsed from the bench onto his knees, clawing in pain at his right eye. Danny could hear the squeals of delight from Mattie as he reeled away before racing into the school building.

"Toby, I'll get you first aid but first of all I'll get hold of Doubty... leave it to me!" exclaimed Danny who was livid with Mattie.

"No, no... leave it Danny. Leave him, I mean... that's exactly what he wants, just help me to first aid," sobbed Toby.

Reluctantly, he did as instructed by his best friend but for Danny, this was too much. Mattie Doubty had gone too far – again. Things may have been improving with the twins and his mum might even get on with their mother but Mattie Doubty needed bringing down a peg or two and Danny Bowen decided he was just the boy for the job.

Danny had tried so hard to change his ways and was proud of how he'd done but he had to now act. Whilst Danny had stepped back from confrontation in the past, he realised that continuing with this approach in relation to Mattie would not work.

As the school week progressed, relations in class were as frosty as the winter weather itself. The snow slowly transformed into an unwelcome slush, followed by puddles of dirty water before finally evaporating in the warming temperature. All the while, Danny plotted his revenge. Suspecting Toby would try to dissuade him, Danny thought things through in isolation and didn't let on to Toby at all.

But it was Thursday breaktime when the situation took a turn for the worse... much worse. The class had been unsettled during Maths, which Miss Patel put down to tiredness, seeing as it was the final couple of days before the spring half-term.

But it was more than that. Danny felt it.

He clearly heard the stifled giggles and gasps from his classmates. It was clear to all that the twins were at their most disruptive and unpleasant, with both involved in many whispered conversations. However, none of these conversations involved Danny, Delilah or Toby.

Feeling unsettled and on edge, Danny headed out for breaktime munching on a piece of toast bought from the tuckshop. Sitting on a playground bench to finish his snack, he looked up to see Lucy reluctantly approaching him. Looking beyond her, he noticed at least five other pupils looking on, as well as the twins themselves. Even before Lucy uttered a word, Danny could feel the blood begin to drain from his head and his heart felt suddenly heavier.

"Go on then, ask him!" snarled Mattie at Lucy, from somewhere within a growing crowd of faces.

"I bet he denies it but he'll be lying," Millie added viciously before Lucy cleared her throat.

"Danny..." she hesitated before continuing, "is it true that your dad isn't even allowed in Shropshire because he beats everyone up, including your mum?"

It was said. And that sentence couldn't now be *'unsaid'*!

The sheer horror of that simple question, coupled with the baying faces in the swelling crowd, momentarily paralysed Danny. He could barely comprehend the question, let alone reply to her. He felt betrayed. All over again. His world literally crumbling before his very eyes, his past – or rather his father's past – once again catching up with him. He felt haunted and still no response. He simply stared back at Lucy, slowly shaking his head and fighting back the tears which he could feel beginning to well up in the corners of his eyes. The incredibly tense atmosphere was suddenly shattered by Mattie Doubty, as he stepped forward from the crowd with a look of delight and hatred etched on his face.

Poking a finger in Danny's direction, he angrily spouted yet more provocative words.

"Told you so..." he triumphantly announced to the watching crowd, "just... look... at... that... guilty... face!"

The next five seconds were played out in slow-motion in Danny's mind. He felt a gut-wrenching sickness as his instincts kicked in. He knew what was about to unfold and almost seemed to be viewing events from on high – as if a spectator rather than one of the main protagonists.

Without a moment's hesitation, he raced towards Mattie – shoving Lucy roughly out of the way in the process. Mattie's sneer quickly turned to a look of panic as he took a rushed and clumsy step backwards but it was too late. Danny was upon him. Grabbing Mattie in a headlock, he wrestled him towards the playground floor. If anything, his rage now seemed even greater, seeing as he had hold of Mattie, than it was moments before. And it was this uncontrollable rage that sealed his fate. Forming his right hand into a tight fist, Danny swung from far behind his back. Contact was almost immediate, as were the consequences. His fist met the middle of Mattie's nose and a split-second later, blood was gushing uncontrollably from Mattie's face onto the tarmac.

The commotion had alerted both Mr Fowler and Mrs Owen, who raced up to the onlooking crowd. Mrs Owen escorted a distraught Mattie for urgent first aid, as Mr Fowler marched Danny unceremoniously to the headteacher's office.

The following sixty minutes were the worst for Danny – sat in perfect isolation outside Mr Stanley's office, whilst his headteacher was in a meeting. Not a soul spoke to him. Nothing from Mr Fowler, other than the instruction to take a seat and go nowhere. Sitting diagonally across from Mrs Richards, she chose not to even make eye contact with him, never mind talk to him. It was this familiar feeling of the soon-to-be-delivered consequences which left Danny feeling desperately low. As bitter tears quietly formed and trickled down his cheeks, he felt that all the good work and his fresh start at Northernvale had been for absolutely nothing.

However, he was still hugely confused as well as upset and angry. How could the Doubty twins have possibly known about Danny's father? He had not mentioned anything to anybody since arriving in Shropshire. Not even his best friends. As this conundrum began to dominate Danny's thoughts, he slowly pieced the jigsaw together. The only plausible way the twins could have known was via their mother, who was now, very clearly, Danny's mum's best friend! He felt betrayed. He hoped that he had jumped to the wrong conclusion but was also a bright enough boy to realise the damage this would potentially do to the trust and bond which he had with his mother.

Lost in thought, Danny was soon jolted back to the present as Mr Stanley opened his door swiftly before slowly shaking his head and inviting Danny to take a seat in his office. Mrs Richards was already there, with a notepad and pen in hand, leaving Danny to wonder how she had slipped past him into the head's office.

Mr Stanley wasn't angry.

He felt let down by Danny and strangely, that made Danny feel even more miserable. He was invited to give his side of the events and his explanation was accompanied by feverish scribbling from Mrs Richards into the notepad. Danny was relieved when his headteacher explained that he was sympathetic to the goading he had received. He also promised Danny that there would be a suitable consequence for Mattie Doubty. Inevitably, Mr Stanley went on to explain how the situation was far more serious for Danny, considering his *'violent and uncontrolled response'*, as Mr Stanley phrased it.

The remainder of that day was spent working at a table

placed outside Mr Stanley's office. Danny knew that more significant consequences were to follow but was pleased to have Toby's company for a few brief moments at the end of dinnertime, whilst eating his lunch in the dinner hall. Toby explained that whilst Mattie was OK, he had gone home because of his injuries. This was a consolation of sorts for Danny, whose actions were now beginning to sink in.

The only communication that afternoon was Mrs Richards explaining that Danny would be met by his mother after school, ahead of a second meeting with Mr Stanley. The remainder of that day was a painful experience for Danny, as the minutes ticked by so slowly. The waiting, Danny considered, was possibly worse than the consequences – whatever they may be!

Whilst the pupils headed home, he was forced to sit for a further ten minutes. As the school emptied and a hush descended on the building Danny felt quite uncomfortable in the knowledge that he was the only pupil in the building. With staff busying themselves, heading here and there, he pondered why teachers needed to even be in school if there were no children to teach.

Eventually, his mother arrived looking both flustered and upset. There was no opportunity for a conversation, as Mrs Richards immediately showed them both into Mr Stanley's office. He was already sitting behind his desk, waiting, arms crossed, eyebrows raised.

"Thank you for attending this meeting Rachel. We know you're upset with what has happened in school earlier today and we appreciate you'll also need time to discuss matters with your son, after this meeting. However, I'd like to start the meeting with you Danny. You need to explain your actions, so that your mother can appreciate your viewpoint."

Danny thought it odd that Mr Stanley referred to his mum by her first name and desperately hoped that it may somehow mean that he was more understanding of the situation, before deciding on a consequence.

Danny did as requested. He did not lie. He did not look to make excuses for his actions. He explained it just as it had been. All the while, his mum sat in silence, listening intently. Danny explained the events in Maths and then the violent, playground incident. It was at this point that he caught sight of his mother dabbing her eyes to dry the tears, as she slowly shook her head. By the end of Danny's explanation, he felt a sense of relief but also shame at his actions. He knew he had let everyone down – especially those in the room and Miss Patel, of course.

"Is Mattie OK, Mr Stanley?" asked Danny's mum, eventually.

"Well, he went home early but we do expect him to be back in school tomorrow. But with a very sore nose!"

"I'm so sorry Mr Stanley. I know I shouldn't have done it but I just lost it... I've tried so hard not to..." Danny's voice trailed off, as he felt more emotional especially seeing the impact on his mother.

"How do we move forward from here?" interrupted Rachel.

Danny's headteacher leafed through some paperwork before selecting a sheet which he appeared to refer to.

"Danny will provide a full, written apology to Mattie and Mattie will apologise both for his actions and unkind words. However, that'll wait until after half-term. Considering his aggressive reaction, I have decided that Danny will also receive a one-day, fixed-term exclusion and this therefore means that he will not attend school tomorrow. In addition, his teacher will talk to the class tomorrow, about this incident."

To Danny, the remainder of the meeting seemed less important – the simple fact was that, just like the bad old days, he wasn't wanted in his school.

CHAPTER 6

No words were exchanged between mother and son as they made the short journey home. Danny was determined to keep the tears at bay as he headed straight up to his bedroom.

It was an hour later that his mum knocked and entered his room. It was also clear to Danny that his mother had shed just as many tears downstairs, as he had in that sixty-minute period. They hugged each other in silence, Rachel holding her son tight, aware too, that their unique bond was about to be tested.

"I'm so sorry mum. I wish I hadn't done it and I'm worried about seeing Miss Patel but I was so angry... so angry with *him*," Danny offered, incapable of even uttering his neighbour's name.

"I know you regret what you did and this won't be like any of your old schools, Danny. You can get back on track, you will get back on track. You have to."

Danny's mother paused but then continued when it was obvious that Danny had nothing to add.

"There's also something I need to tell you, Danny..."

"You don't need to go on mum," interrupted Danny, "you told the neighbour about dad, didn't you?"

After an audible sigh, Danny's mum confirmed that this was the case.

Danny gently pushed his mum away from him before averting his gaze from her and silently folding his arms, in protest. Staring into the middle distance he asked a rhetorical question of his mother.

"Why is it that you'd share something like this with basically not much more than a stranger? I don't want anybody to know about my dad. I'm ashamed of him and now the whole world knows everything. Thank you, mum," he added, sarcastically.

Another apology was offered but it fell on deaf ears – Danny was then relieved to see his mother vacate his room. He needed time to come to terms with the day's events.

It was the Friday morning of Danny's one-day exclusion before the two spoke again, this time at the breakfast table. It was almost the start of the school day but Danny was still dressed in his pyjamas, sitting in abject misery. He heard the Doubty's front door slam closed and briefly caught sight of the twins as they walked past the lounge window on their way to school. That simple sighting brought emotions of anger and regret to the fore again.

"Oh, Danny, don't upset yourself. I'm so sorry about all of this," his mum said trying to soothe her son.

He simply stood up and returned to his room. He found himself further frustrated by the fact his djembe drum was still in school. Focusing on his drumming would have provided a welcome distraction.

With Rachel's shift due to start at the shop at 10am, she knew she had to prioritise her family, especially with relations in such a fragile state. The wages lost would be a blow to the family's finances but the chance to re-establish trust was worth so much more than a couple of hours pay. After a quick phone call to the shop, Danny's mum headed back upstairs determined to repair the damage. As she entered, it was Danny who spoke first.

"I am really sorry mum; I know I let everybody down but I can't change what happened."

"I'm glad that you understand you've done wrong and I also hope that you understand that you can't continue to use your fists like this. You and I know more than most, the damage that can be done when people resort to using violence. It scares me that you won't learn this lesson and I can't even begin to think of what will happen if you don't see sense, Danny," she finished.

More tears between the two but more importantly an embrace. An embrace which signalled that trust could begin to be restored between the duo. Danny knew his mum was right, no matter the level of provocation, he'd made the wrong choice.

"Do you forgive me for telling Rebecca, Danny?"

"Of course I do. I love you, mum."

Normality was returning and they were both thankful for that. Danny's mum disappeared for ten minutes, returning with school work for Danny to complete – as well as handing over his djembe drum.

"Thanks, mum," Danny said whilst smiling for the first time in over a day. This now meant Danny had his drum over half-term and that would provide a welcome distraction and focus for him. As it turned out, Danny was happy for his mum to return to the shop to complete the last two hours of her shift, which would certainly help a little. Before heading out, his mum made him a cup of tea and dug out a couple of biscuits. The two of them often laughed about his passion for tea and biscuits. Danny's mum would joke that it sometimes felt like living with an old man and she didn't pass up this opportunity to remind her son, once again.

As Danny sipped his tea and dunked his biscuits, he figured that at least one consolation to this whole episode would be that Mattie Doubty would never mock him again. This was tempered with the fact that so many in school now knew about the most difficult aspect of Danny's life before his move to Shropshire. This thought lingered, just as another entered his head... the loft!

Of course. The shared loft. If Mattie Doubty could invade Danny Bowen's privacy, then why can't Danny Bowen return the favour?

This unexpected question, which Danny had posed to himself, led to him quickly washing up his cup before collecting the stepladders from the back garden shed. A familiar ritual was beginning again. A short while later, Danny was scrambling back up into the loft and moments later he stood stock-still – his feet firmly planted on the boundary of his loft space and that of his neighbour's. He inhaled deeply, exhaled and strode forward into unchartered waters. He figured he had no more than thirty minutes, so set to work immediately. It was a far simpler search than the school loft as it wasn't an especially big area, maybe the size of a small bedroom, plus there were just five or six boxes to root through.

Just like most items consigned to the loft, Danny unearthed: old clothes, toys, books, magazines and even a battered old pair of army-themed, walkie-talkies. On first inspection there didn't seem much else on offer but Danny knew of the merits of digging deeper and persevering. Moments later, he was rewarded. At the base of the 'fifth box' Danny spotted what looked like a wooden, treasure chest or maybe even a memory box. After tugging it free from the larger box, he noticed a lock on the front panel. The shoebox-shaped chest was locked but conveniently, the intricately-designed, metal key was sitting in the lock itself! A simple anti-clockwise, quarter-turn later and the top popped open. Danny was clever enough to know that special items were placed in attractive chests such as the one in his hands now. It was exactly what he'd been looking for and maybe it was about to reveal a special secret, for Danny's eyes only. His hopes were quickly realised. It came in the form of two cards and a newspaper clipping, all securely stored at the base of the chest.

With time ticking and Danny unearthing something he could possibly use against the twins, he felt his heart beat that little bit more quickly, with the excitement and anticipation. Both cards were small but identical in size. He carefully placed them side by side, then shifted his body position so he wasn't blocking the light. The first card had an illustration of flowers on the front and the second, an image of a springer spaniel dog. He opened both cards and read each message in turn.

Dear Daddy,
I miss you.
Love,
Millie. xxxxx
Then:
To Daddy,
You're the best.
Love,
Mattie. xxxxx

It was clear to Danny, despite the toddler-style handwriting, that each card was signed by one of the twins. He had never actually seen the twins' dad and had wondered where he was. As he carefully unfolded the newspaper article, Danny quickly realised why there was no father! He read, then reread every single word of the newspaper clipping. As he reread it, he felt his anger towards both Mattie and Millie slowly dissipate.

Marcus Doubty had been a soldier – a dog handler, with the British Army. At the age of twenty-seven, and with the twins barely four years old, Marcus and his springer spaniel dog, had been killed by an explosive device, concealed under the surface of a dirt track, in Afghanistan.

For the second time in successive days, Danny felt sick to

the pit of his stomach. His own father was, in Danny's view, an awful father but at least he wasn't dead! His desire to learn more about Mattie's past had led Danny down a path on which he now wished he'd never embarked. Quickly putting everything back in its place, Danny clambered out of the loft, just in time so as not to arouse suspicions from his returning mother.

That following weekend was one of reflection for Danny and what made matters worse, was that he felt there was nobody he could turn to for advice, other than possibly his mother. Toby and Delilah were his best mates but he knew they wouldn't approve of what he had got up to since his exclusion. And what if he did share this with them and they then revealed this secret at a later date?

Danny's past was difficult, it was unfair and it had been hard too. But it hadn't been tragic, unlike children who lose their father forever when only four years old, just as the Doubty twins had done so.

Again, he considered talking to his mother. After all, he had never withheld anything from her in the past. They were usually inseparable. Whatever life threw at them, they came through it - together. Then there was the question whether she already knew. And if she did, why hadn't she shared it with him? Especially when he considered how the twins had revealed his secret in such a public way!

Contradictory thoughts tormented Danny for the next two days, he could only sleep for short periods and felt listless when awake, like a ship lost at sea.

Luckily, Danny didn't have to wait too long to be rescued by a familiar source later that week.

"Dan, you've been so distant since the weekend. Something's on your mind. Please tell me?" asked his mother.

"It's that fight with Mattie…" Danny replied, half-heartedly before he was interrupted.

"No, it's not Danny. It's more than that. I know it is... we know each other so well, so please be truthful with me. We have nothing, if we don't have that," she said, with hesitation and concern in her voice.

Danny felt a knot forming in the pit of his stomach but knew he had to come clean.

"I went back in the loft the other day, mum. I wanted to do to Mattie what he did to me. I wanted to know about his past. Like he knows about our past. So, I did and now I know."

There was no response from his mother which surprised Danny. So, he continued.

"The loft's weird. I think I told you. Basically, you can go into anybody's loft space – so I went into Millie and Mattie's. Just looking. Looking for anything."

His mother simply nodded, confirming she understood what Danny was saying whilst encouraging him to further elaborate.

"I wanted to know secrets about him. He knows our biggest secret and he shared it with everyone in school. And I found one mum but I wish I hadn't!"

At this point the tears made an untimely return.

"What is it that you found, Danny? Are you telling me you know about their father?"

That second question caught Danny with his guard down.

"What? What d'you mean mum?"

"That he's not around for them?" she replied.

"Yeah... that he was killed when they were young," confirmed Danny, quietly.

"I knew already Danny. Rebecca told me a few weeks ago. I like her Danny. She opened up to me. She explained how much she loved and now misses her husband. That is why I told her about your father."

Danny now fully understood the reasoning behind his

mother sharing their secret with Rebecca and also the reason behind them leaving Liverpool, nine months earlier. That reason now suddenly seemed far less important than it had before Danny had located the cards and clipping in the Doubty's loft.

"You know, I do regret that Rebecca shared details about your father with her children. She regrets it too, obviously but what's done is done. Rebecca wants to apologise to you Danny, but now that you know their secret, I think it changes things but I'm not quite sure how!"

Danny slept better that night. He had cleared the air with his mother and the trust between them had been fully restored. Whilst he was owed an apology from Rebecca, he too needed to now return the favour. It was his mum who suggested it first. A meal out with the Doubty family!

"Have you gone crazy mum? A meal out with the three of them!"

"It's not as crazy as it seems, Danny. Think about it. If you could demonstrate to school that you'd made things up with Mattie, in particular, then that would reflect well on you. And, far more importantly, you also need to apologise to Mattie for invading his privacy *and* for punching him on the nose," she finished.

"What and he doesn't owe me an apology?" replied Danny.

"Yes, of course he does and I'm sure he'd want to do that and wipe the slate clean."

After the briefest of moments, he responded to his mother.

"Well, it's up to you mum. I do feel like I need to speak to Mattie and Millie about what I discovered," added Danny, before flicking the TV set on. Focusing on the television was his way of leaving the final decision up to his mother.

Rachel took the hint, and left her son to his own devices, heading next door to discuss the proposal with Rebecca. No more than twenty minutes later she returned.

The meeting was on. Rebecca was keen to build bridges and had already explained to Mattie and Millie about Danny's visit to their loft space. So after a whirlwind morning, the mums had set up lunch at the village pub that midweek afternoon of half-term.

"This is so weird, mum," uttered Danny as he squirmed uncomfortably on the pub's leather sofa. "But I suppose it'll help to move on with the twins. If I can learn to just put up with them, then at least I won't end up punching Mattie again," added Danny, nervously.

"How do you think Toby and Delilah will react if you do make it up with the twins, Danny?"

The question remained unanswered, other than Danny raising an eyebrow. At that moment, Millie popped her head around the corner and it was Danny who made eye contact with her first. She smiled warmly as she walked tentatively over to them. Moments later, Mattie and Rebecca joined them. Mattie's body language was in contrast to that of his sister's. He looked both uneasy and awkward and as if he'd rather be anywhere else in the world at that particular moment. Danny was relieved he had got to the pub first, figuring it was harder to walk into a room when everybody else was there. Strangely, Mattie's awkwardness had the opposite effect on Danny, making him feel more comfortable. With this added reassurance, he decided to make the first move.

He stood up. Leaning towards Mattie, he offered his hand, asking his neighbour if they could be *'mates'*.

Mattie's tense demeanour evaporated in the blink of an eye, and as they shook hands he smiled from ear to ear and nodded his acceptance of Danny's proposal. There followed a series of apologies, so many in fact that it bordered on the comical. The mood was further lightened when Danny's mum apologised to Millie, even though it was agreed that there was no need for the apology in the first place!

To Danny, this felt like the seedling of an almost unimaginable relationship, with a most unexpected duo.

The mains and pudding were delicious and delivered in a timely fashion, meaning that within an hour of arriving, the dining was over. As both mums ordered coffees and mints, Mattie took the opportunity to ask if Danny could come back to their home. A couple of minutes later the boys and Millie were back at the house.

As Danny stepped into the lounge, he instantly spotted the same keep-sake chest from the loft, this time placed on the lounge coffee table. Sitting alongside it were what appeared to be three family albums. For the briefest of moments Danny felt defensive, as if this was all set up to catch him out.

"Danny, can me and Mattie show you pictures of our dad, please?" Millie asked softly.

"Err... yeah, of course. You must miss him Millie? I bet he was a good dad. Was he strong?" continued Danny, with comments and questions spilling out of his mouth, "in the newspaper photograph, he looked like he had big muscles... that's why I ask if he was strong," continued Danny, keen to talk through any periods of silence.

"Yeah he was," interrupted Mattie, "and his dog, Meg, was lovely too! We want to share our memories of our dad with you, Danny. It'll help us and it would be good to sort of try and make up for the way we treated you in school, the other week," he finished.

So, they spent the next hour talking about Marcus and leafing through one picture after another. It was clear to Danny that they had so many happy, vivid memories to look back on - from Christmases to holidays and everything in-between.

Only on one occasion did Millie become visibly upset, when explaining that her father's tour was three weeks from finishing on the day her father and Meg were killed by the explosion. The room fell quiet for the briefest of moments but Mattie's warm embrace of his sister had the desired effect. In that one simple act, Danny witnessed love and empathy from Mattie towards his sister, which he would previously have questioned whether Mattie was even capable of!

As Millie turned the page, the mood lifted again. Staring out from the album were the grinning faces of Marcus and Millie. Dad crouched alongside his daughter – who was strapped securely in a high chair – both plastered from just below the eyes to the bottom of the chin in what appeared to be strawberry yogurt. The three of them laughed in unison.

Sharing in their memories enabled Danny to reconsider everything he had previously thought about the twins. He had been suspicious and distrustful of them. He knew better now. They were open and they were kind. With every page they turned together, he felt a warmth and a bond with the duo which took him by surprise. The barriers that he had placed between himself and the twins, simply disappeared, one by one. He realised too, how much love they still had for their father but that was tinged with sadness and the knowledge they would never see, speak or hug him again. Danny felt so much empathy towards Mattie and Millie and was therefore happy to be as open with them as they had been with him, when Millie asked a question which suddenly turned the tables.

"Was your dad sometimes kind too?"

Danny smiled, remembering that sometimes that had indeed been the case.

"Yeah Millie, he was. Just depended on the mood he was in. I remember having fun with him but I don't think I loved him as much as you two loved your dad. Mainly because… because he could be so cruel to mum…" continued Danny, failing to elaborate any further. The twins sensed it was best probably not to ask any further questions.

"Anyway, at least every memory of your dad is a positive one and you've got so much in this box and these pictures to remind you of him."

Mattie was next to speak.

"Yeah, thanks Danny. Me and Millie have got loads of camera footage too, with all four of us. They're the best 'cos they bring dad back to life. We don't need to imagine how he talked, how he walked. We just watch, don't we Millie?"

"We do but not very often because mum always ends up in tears when we watch the footage together and even though she says they're *'happy'* tears, me and Mattie aren't sure," finished Millie.

"I'd love to watch them with you another day if that's OK?" replied Danny.

As Millie nodded, the three of them spotted both mums walking past the lounge window.

"I'll be getting off then. Maybe we could meet later this week? I'm not up to much," said Danny as he strained to squeeze his feet into his trainers.

"That'd be good," replied Millie on behalf of the two of them, as they said their goodbyes.

CHAPTER 7

"Tea and biscuits, old man?" asked mum, as Danny slipped his trainers off and flicked them into the corner of the hall with his feet.

"Oh, go on then, mum. Let's live life on the edge!" grinned Danny as he sat himself on the end of the kitchen table. The next half hour slipped by with easy conversation between the two of them. Danny promised that he would never judge a book by its cover again, accepting that he had done this in relation to the twins.

In his defence, Danny's mother did explain that this was understandable when considering that many people, in the form of teachers, school staff and peers, had judged Danny in previous years before even getting to know him.

"But two wrongs don't make a right, mum. And now that I've made friends with Mattie and Millie, I can go back to school next week and tell Miss Patel, Mrs Owen and Mr Stanley that things are sorted!"

Rachel smiled and said nothing. Only her son could turn such a negative into a positive. But that was Danny through and through, and that was why she was so proud of him.

Whilst Danny didn't catch up with the twins for the remainder of that week, he did take the time to go to Delilah's on the Friday, where he also caught up with Toby. Explaining Wednesday's events to the two of them and how he had changed his viewpoint so much, was trickier than Danny had anticipated.

"So, what are you telling us Danny?" began Delilah, "that

your best mates aren't us two now but the twins instead?"

Danny explained again. That it was about friendships, not *'best mates'*. Arriving in Shropshire nine months earlier, Danny had been fortunate to make friends with the likes of Toby and Delilah and he was reminded of this once again, as his friends' tones softened and after a few more minutes they appeared to be accepting of Danny's news.

"OK, Danny. I think we've got it. Look, it'll be strange to make an effort with the two of them but we're cool with it. We'll give it a go," smiled Toby as he replied on behalf of both of them.

"At least we won't need to worry about you punching Mattie again," added Delilah helpfully.

"Exactly! I thought that too," laughed Danny.

The rest of that half-term holiday ticked by in a rather uneventful manner. Danny was looking forward to school again, safe in the knowledge that the added complication of the twins, was something he would no longer need to worry about. Over that second weekend, he found himself pondering his experience in the school loft again.

What had the lady wanted?
And if he could work that out, could he help her?
Would he see her again?
Did he want to see her again?

As these questioned floated aimlessly around Danny's mind, the only thing he was sure of, was that somehow his beloved drum held the answer but then how could an inanimate object provide the answer? Yet another question!

Sure enough, Monday morning soon came around. On his way to school Danny calculated that more than half of the school year had now elapsed and considered if the second half of year 6 would be anywhere near as eventful as the first half.

"Hello again, Miss," Danny greeted his teacher with a trademark smile, before continuing, "we need to stop meeting like this, on the playground on the first day of each half-term!"

Humour was the best way for Danny to deal with that first exchange with his teacher, since his exclusion before the half-term holiday.

It worked, as Miss Patel laughed.

"I see you've not misplaced that wicked sense of humour of yours over the holiday, Danny!"

"Thanks, Miss. I am sorry about the fight I had with Mattie. Could I please talk to you at breaktime? I've got something I need to tell you."

"Of course you can."

And they did, for the whole of breaktime.

It was only the familiar sound of the bell signalling the end of break, that brought an abrupt end to the conversation. It had though been long enough to explain that, with the help of his mother, he had managed to heal the wounds with the twins. Miss Patel had complimented Danny on using his initiative and maturity in finding such a positive way in which to move forward.

Later that day, Danny was called to Mr Stanley's office. It quickly became apparent to Danny that Miss Patel and Mr Stanley had been in conversation about him.

It's clear to me…" began Mr Stanley, "just by your actions, that you've already learnt a great deal from your one-day exclusion. That gives me encouragement for the rest of the school year. I'm sure it'll be trouble-free."

"It will, Mr Stanley. Sometimes you've gotta be in a really sad place to learn something. Not being allowed into my school on that Friday was horrible. I don't want to be there again."

As the conversation continued, Danny was reassured that in Mr Stanley, he had a headteacher who understood and cared about him and the decisions he made. Mr Stanley even took the time to explain that school life hadn't been easy for him. At primary school, he had often been poorly behaved and that he was even put on report at secondary school. This helped Danny even further. His headteacher hadn't needed to share that with him but by doing so, he had demonstrated the trust and belief that he had in Danny, for the remainder of the school year. As he returned to class, Danny made a promise to himself. He wouldn't share what Mr Stanley had just admitted about his own experiences. Not with Miss Patel nor even his mother.

Danny's only regret in his exchange with his headteacher was that he wasn't brave enough to raise the topic of the ghostly figure, witnessed some months previously. Maybe some things are best left alone, he considered, as he turned the door handle and re-entered his classroom.

The following day and *'just to make sure'* as Miss Patel phrased it, she asked to meet with Danny, Toby, Delilah, Mattie and Millie. For Danny, it was reassuring that Northernvale Primary was a school that truly cared about him and all of its pupils.

"As a school, we want you all to be *'peaceful, problem-solvers'* and I have to confess I've never seen a better example of it in action. So please, let's not go back to where we were two weeks ago," finished Miss Patel. The smiles around the table provided the confirmation the class teacher was looking for and the following fortnight in school was both enjoyable and harmonious for all.

Wrekin Class benefitted from Mr Stanley's company for the weekly drumming sessions. Their headteacher, being no shrinking violet, loved being part of the action. Miss Patel provided him with one of the spare djembe drums and he asked if he could be just a step or two behind Danny for the drumming procession on the 1st July. The class rejoiced and cheered loudly when Miss Patel informed him that he'd be bringing up the rear!

The pupils did though, have to acknowledge the speed at which Mr Stanley developed his drumming skills, performing with a fair degree of confidence and ability in a short space of time.

With his headteacher being a regular fixture in his class, Danny toyed, once again, with the idea of mentioning the ghostly figure in the loft. His need to ask the question was too great to ignore. So, he took his opportunity at hometime on the Friday afternoon, after yet another drumming session. As he quietly approached Mr Stanley, he was still unsure as to how he would actually frame the question.

"Mr Stanley, you're a great drummer... I mean, you're as good as anyone else and you've got to that level so quick. I'm just pleased we got the drums out of the school loft in the first place!"

Danny paused but couldn't help himself, before continuing.

"Getting that last drum was a bit weird though wasn't it? I mean, it's difficult to explain what *we* saw, isn't it?"

There. It was done. Danny stopped dead. And waited. And waited.

"Danny, when you get to my age..." now it was the headteacher's turn to pause, "there's nothing weird or unusual about hurting your back!"

Danny felt his heart sink at this reply. Why couldn't he just admit what he saw, so that they could both talk about it together?

"Anyway, since then I've had physio on it, so fingers crossed it won't reoccur. Have a lovely weekend, Danny. See you Monday."

And with that, Mr Stanley walked away. A feeling of frustration and confusion briefly overwhelmed Danny, to the point that he actually began to question whether he had really seen a ghost or not. But then, what he remembered as vividly as the ghost itself, was the silent look the pair of them exchanged, when they both realised there was a third entity with them in the loft. No words were required at that point and Danny knew for sure that his headteacher had seen exactly what he had seen too. Either way, there was little point in raising the matter with his headteacher again. Danny knew he had to move on, move forward. And he would have to do this alone.

Early the following week, Miss Patel somewhat burst the bubble of positivity in Wrekin Class, as she was the messenger of some sad news.

"You'll all recall our Christmas Carol visit to the old folks' home and meeting with Harold and Dot, two of our former pupils?" she asked. "Sadly, over the weekend, Harold passed away peacefully," Miss Patel added, to the accompaniment of two or three quiet gasps from the children.

"It is sad news, Wrekin Class but these things inevitably happen and the timing is unfortunate when you consider his link to our school. I think we ought to send a card to Harold's family and maybe we could visit all the residents once again?"

The children were keen on both proposals and it was Toby who reminded Danny, at breaktime, about their flippant remarks relating to Harold and Dot when they had met a couple of months earlier.

"It's strange to think we'll not see him and it'll be just Dot on the 1st July, it's sad really," mused Toby.

For Danny, it was a chance to reflect on how difficult it must continue to be for Millie and Mattie. Here was Toby – sad that a very frail and elderly man he'd only met once, had died. Therefore, how much harder must it be for the twins to have lost their father the way they had?

The news seemed to enable the class to harness even more energy and positivity into their drumming, that afternoon. In addition, it was the other preparations: such as mask-making, along with creating numerous 'centenary-celebration' banners and flags to festoon around the school, ahead of July, which really moved up a gear or two.

The school year continued to march on relentlessly. The days were noticeably drawing out, the animals – especially the birds, Danny thought, were operating at full volume, particularly with their bright chirping at dawn each morning.

Mr Stanley's Monday morning assembly focused on another welcome sign of spring knocking on the door. The delicate snowdrops had already blossomed into full bloom in the forest school area with the daffodils and bluebells not too far behind. Such beautiful glimpses of nature had previously gone unnoticed by Danny but served to remind him of how lucky he felt he was to be in a school, a community and a village which now felt like home to him.

But situations rarely stay the same for too long though and it was two or three weeks later, in early March that Danny was reminded of this, the moment he spotted it.

Somewhere, from the deep recesses of his mind, he knew he'd seen it before but where? Standing stock-still, focusing intently on a blue car parked outside his home, he felt that first shiver. The slightest of shivers to begin with but one that ran down the length of his spine. Moments later the penny dropped. He linked the car to its owner. To their family's social worker.

CHAPTER 8

"NO…NO…NO…" shouted Danny, out of fear, frustration and to nobody in particular. He knew well enough that a visit from the social worker – as nice as she was – would bring an unwelcome intrusion into his life, when everything was going just fine. Much, much better than fine, in fact.

He instinctively turned on his heels and took ten or so strides back towards school before coming to a halt for a second time. So many questions. So many ifs and buts! If he just walked in the opposite direction and returned in three hours or so, it would be OK. The car would have gone and things would be back to how they should be.

But wouldn't his mum need him at home now?
Why had the social worker turned up out of the blue?

The questions tumbled out of the mid-afternoon sky, down onto Danny like a great weight, pinning him to the spot. At this point his instincts kicked in. He loved his mother and needed to be there for her, whatever news awaited him. So he turned, one more time facing his home and that car. He took a deep breath and found that his feet carried him forward in more of a jog than a walk. He stepped through the front door and as anticipated, was greeted by a smile from a familiar face.

The social worker asked Danny to sit down. As he did so he glanced briefly at his mother who was wearing a guarded look.

"What's going on, Julie? Why are you here? And before you say a word, there's no chance you are moving me or mum from this house and I'm not returning to Liverpool. No way!"

"Danny. Please relax. I'm certainly not suggesting you move from Northernvale or this house..." she began by way of a reply. Danny heard little after this opening response, such was the feeling of relief. It felt as if Julie had spoken for a minute or so and it was only when she addressed him by name, that he refocused on her.

"So, Danny, what do you think?" she asked again. Of course, he had no idea what she was talking about. Rachel retreated to the kitchen to make a cup of tea for them and Julie followed. She asked that Rachel talk with Danny about the proposal and then get back to her. It was agreed, ahead of Julie saying her goodbyes and leaving Danny and his mother alone. They sat together on the sofa, tea in hand as his mother explained.

"The long and the short of it Danny, is that this has to be a decision you make for yourself. It's not my decision to make for you."

Inevitably, it was all about Danny's father – what else could it be?

He had done everything demanded and asked of him by the courts and social services, ever since they'd left their home the previous summer. So now he wanted to return – he wanted to be part of the family once more.

Danny's thoughts were dominated by that frightening, final night when he last saw his dad being dragged away from the home into a waiting police car. He found it hard to figure out how you could go from there, to where they were supposedly now. And all in little more than ten months. What Danny and his mother both had to accept, like it or not, was that he had done the right thing since the previous summer.

Danny's mother went on to explain that Julie had phoned

earlier that day and travelled down from Liverpool, arriving at midday.

"Your dad wants us *both* to forgive him, Danny. He wants to move down to live with us here. I can't forgive him for what he did to me and I don't think I ever will be able to. Your father and I have no future together. I explained this to Julie and she understood."

"Well, that's it then, isn't it? You've made my decision for me too," he added.

"Well, Julie said that she expected me to want nothing to do with your father. So did he, I think... because Julie went on to ask specifically about you. That was the question she asked you Danny! If your father can't move in with us, he still wants a relationship with you. He wants to make things up with you and be a *'proper'* dad, is how Julie phrased it when we were talking earlier."

"No chance mum! Why would I ever want to see him again? Especially after he treated you as badly as he did. We're a team, mum. It's both of us or neither of us and also, I've got used to not having him around. He's no loss."

All of what Danny said was somewhere near the truth of his real feelings. Other than that final sentence. Sometimes he did think about his dad, especially since that conversation with the twins at half-term. Danny's mum explained that Julie didn't need to know immediately and took the opportunity to change the topic of conversation back to school. Danny's father was not mentioned that evening, or indeed that weekend. However, in his own company, Danny spent a great deal of time thinking about his father. He found himself resenting him all over again.

That next week at school was trickier for him. Danny found it difficult to focus on anything for any period of time. No sooner had he thought he was winning that inner battle in his mind, then his father's proposition would return. He would see the blue car and Julie too. He got through the remainder of the school week as best as he could. His mother, true to her word, was there for him but also giving him the time and space to make his own decision.

However, that Friday evening, Danny's mother once again raised the subject.

"Look, Danny – I can see how difficult this is for you. But you must make a decision for yourself. Please don't say no to meeting your father, if it's to protect me or out of loyalty to me. I'm big enough to stand on my own two feet. It must be what you want to do and you alone."

There was no response from Danny and he was slightly surprised to see her starting to root through her handbag.

"Here, Danny..." she said whilst holding out a sealed envelope, "this is a letter from your father for you, not me. I didn't give it to you last Friday, as I thought you might destroy it. I really think you should read it. It might help you in making up your mind," she added helpfully.

Once again there were no words from Danny but, as requested, he took the envelope from his mother. Letter in hand, he retreated to his room and gently closed his bedroom door behind himself. Moments later, he unfolded the letter and began to read:

Dear Danny,
Not sure where to start with this. I really should say 'Thank You' for being brave enough to read it. I also want to say SORRY for being such a terrible dad to you and husband to your mum.
You deserve none of what has happened over the last few years. All of this mess is 100% my fault.
It has taken all of this time since you and mum left Liverpool after that night, for me to realise it's all down to me. I am so sorry for that. But I can't tell you how happy and

proud of you I was, when Julie told me how well you are doing in Shropshire.

So, I will understand if you want to carry on with life as it is. So let me say now, if your wish is to never see me again, as hard as that will be to accept, I promise you, on my life, that I will never try to contact you again for as long as I live.

If I could turn the clock back and start again Danny, then I would do it in a heartbeat. There would be nothing more in the world I'd want, than a second chance. The day you were born Danny, was the best day of my life and I've wasted so much time since then. I have made so many bad choices. I have been truly awful to your mum. So here I am, having to write this letter, pleading for you to give me just one more chance. I promise that if you do, you'll not regret it.

Will you please meet me, Danny?

I will never make excuses for my behaviour but I want you to know everything if we can meet. You can ask me anything you like!

Before I wrote this letter, Julie said she could easily arrange things, if you agreed to meet. She could collect you from home and drive you to Liverpool for the day. She could even stay with you while we met. If you did meet me, I can make the same promise again. If you decided you then didn't want to see me again, then I would accept this.

Whether or not I see you again, you will always be my son. Grandma Pat and Grandpa Lenny send their love.

Thank you for reading this letter, Danny.

I love you,

Dad

xxx

Danny immediately reread the letter – every paragraph, line and word. He then gently slid it under his pillow before those familiar emotions of doubt and insecurity took a hold.

Tears flowed freely as Danny had no idea of what to do next.

His mother was quickly alerted to her son's quiet sobbing and was there for him.

"Can I read the letter, Danny? Would that help?" she asked kindly.

"Please," was the one-word response.

He studied his mother intently as she read the letter before she folded it up and carefully returned it to where Danny had retrieved it from.

"Danny. All I have to say is this. What have you got to lose by meeting him?"

"But what if I do and he doesn't keep his promise, mum? What if I meet him and never want to see him again! What then?"

"He will accept your decision, Danny, just like he says in the letter. Whilst your father is not somebody I love anymore; he is a man of his word. Why not sleep on it?" she added.

And so he did.

That following morning, Danny had promised his mother that he would make a decision by the end of the week. She had reminded him that there wasn't a need to place such a tight timeframe on such an important decision and that she would support him whatever course of action he took. Danny's determination to stick to the timings was partly down to the fact that he felt he'd get little opportunity for a good night's sleep, until the decision was made!

The next couple of days passed by with little incident at home or school but Danny was no nearer making a decision, which began to frustrate him all over again.

It was walking to school on the Friday morning of that week when Danny felt the germ of an idea form in his mind. It was obvious to him now, so obvious he kicked himself that it hadn't crossed his mind sooner.

His relationship with the twins was now a strong and positive one. They had shared their memories and pain of losing their father with him. He thought that surely they were best placed to help their new friend. He lost no time. He invited Mattie and Millie to his house straight after school that day. Fortunately, his mum had an afternoon shift at the shop, so he figured that they wouldn't need to talk in whispers. But then again, he thought his mum would probably encourage him to talk to the twins, such was their relationship – quite a contrast to just a few months earlier.

"Thanks for coming over..." Danny began, "I want to talk to both of you about my dad. I need your advice. I could have spoken to Toby and Delilah but you'd get it better than they would, what... with everything that's happened in the past. Will you listen, please?"

Millie immediately nodded, then thanked Danny for feeling like he could talk to them.

"You were both so honest, so open, when we talked about Marcus... I mean your dad. Problem is, I just don't know what to do. Well I think I do but I'm not certain. I want your help with deciding but I'm not being babyish, I'm not going to tell you what I *think* I should do, until I hear your opinions! Is that OK?"

"Anything for a mate!" said Mattie. All three smiled before Millie invited Danny to tell them everything, other than what he thought he should do.

Danny went on to include every detail. Not only the recent social worker visit but he explained to the twins some of his father's most frightening behaviour – including that last night in Liverpool. The twins listened, totally engrossed in Danny's story. After finishing the recount of his troubled past, he handed the letter to Millie for them both to read. Whilst a little hesitant, Millie took the letter from Danny, as Mattie began to read it too, from over his sister's shoulder.

What seemed like an eternity to Danny came to an end as Millie checked her brother had read the letter, before handing it back to Danny.

"Well... what should I do? What would you do?"

"What does your mum reckon, Danny?" asked Mattie.

"I knew you'd ask me that Mattie!" Danny replied. "It doesn't matter – just tell me what you would do, please!"

It was Millie who went first.

"The way your dad has behaved is scary and horrible, Danny. I'm not sure if I would want to meet him, he's been so unkind to your mum. But I suppose he regrets it now. Either that or he is a brilliant liar. I believe him in the letter but I'm sorry, I just don't know... actually, I don't think I'd meet him!" she finished.

"I don't think I agree Millie..." started Mattie, "you've already said that you've got happy memories of your dad, Danny. Surely he wants to make it up to you? I think he is being truthful in the letter too... so if you don't like meeting him then he has promised to leave you alone. So why not? You will have the social worker with you too and what if you never meet him? In ten years, you might regret it and it would be too late! Danny, you're luckier than us. You still have a dad. There's nothing more in the world us two would want, than to see our dad again!"

"Don't forget Meg too, Mattie!" interrupted his sister, adding to the conversation in a very quiet and reflective way.

In his heart of hearts, this is what Danny had been hoping to hear from his friends and for him, it enabled him to finally come to a decision. And that was to give his father one last chance.

"Thanks. I'm gonna meet him!" announced Danny, getting to his feet. Millie smiled, stood too and warmly hugged him. With Mattie, still seated and looking on, it was Danny who spoke next.

"Nice one, mate," Mattie simply said, as the twins headed back home.

This time, it was Danny who had the tea and biscuits prepared for his mum as she returned from work. As Danny dunked his second biscuit and talked, his mother sipped her brew and listened. She smiled and shared with him that she had hoped he would decide to meet his father again. So, it was agreed. Rachel would contact Julie on the Monday to arrange a meeting at the start of the Easter holidays.

CHAPTER 9

That weekend, Danny set aside time to write back to his father ahead of the meeting.

His pen flowed, the moment he sat down at the table. The letter-writing task far easier than he could have imagined.

Hello dad,
I was a bit surprised (well very surprised actually) to get your letter last week. To start with I was angry and annoyed. You made me and mum move from Liverpool and from my friends and then you were writing to me being as nice as pie! I can never forgive you for how you treated my mum. I love her more than anything and you need to know that.
Julie told me you wanted to meet and that you were very sorry. I didn't really know what to do. I spoke to mum and I spoke to two of my best mates. They are actually twins who live next door. So, I have lots of questions to ask you and I don't know if I want you in my life until you have answered them.
I will meet you in Liverpool because I want answers to my questions. Mum will speak to Julie to sort it out.
So, I will see you then.
From,
Danny

Danny chose not to reread his letter, a letter which had taken no more than five minutes to write. He wanted it to be matter-of-fact. He didn't ask his mum to read it, there was no need. He simply folded it neatly, placed it in an envelope, then licked and sealed the envelope flap securely.

Early the following week the letter had been passed on and within a fortnight Danny's mum had been in conversation with Julie and had news for Danny, as he returned home from school on that Friday.

As he opened the front door, he spotted the tea and biscuits awaiting him. He slung his school bag casually from his shoulder and slipped his school shoes off.

"Hi Danny, how was school?"

"Yeah, not bad, thanks. The drumming went well this afternoon and Mr Stanley's really good now – well most of the time. He's better behaved too. Miss didn't tell him off today!" laughed Danny. "In fact, Mattie took the mick out of him when we were drumming. He missed his cue and so everybody was then out of rhythm. Mattie shouted, *'Keep up Stanners!'* and everyone laughed. Miss Patel even said that when he was drumming in class with us, we could call him 'Stanners'. She's really cool mum and Mr Stanley doesn't mind either!"

"Very funny, Danny…" smiled his mother before continuing, "I spoke to Julie earlier today, Danny."

"Oh, go on… what did she say?"

"Well, she can collect you at the beginning of the Easter holidays, which is only around the corner now! She said she could take you to Liverpool and stay with you, I mean in the same room, while you meet your father."

"How long for though?" Danny replied.

"Only an hour, unless you wanted a little longer. She needs to know for definite, Danny. So, are you still prepared to go?"

Danny confirmed that he was. He wanted answers to his questions. Questions he had even started to write down, so as to memorise. Shortly after this brief conversation between the two, the text to Julie had been sent and there was no going back. Danny was one step closer to getting his answers and the scheduled meeting now seemed more real than previously.

Danny turned up for that last week of the spring term in high spirits. His friendships were now built up over time and on solid foundations, he loved his school more than ever and he felt confident enough to think positively about meeting his father.

On the Wednesday of that week, he was one of twelve lucky pupils in Wrekin Class to board the school minibus and head back to the local old folks' home. Also, this time they took a dozen djembe drums with them, after Miss Patel had persuaded the care home matron to allow the pupils to play the drums for the residents' enjoyment. Of course, the visit was tinged with sadness – their teacher had reread the letter about Harold's untimely passing to the class again - that morning. On their arrival, Dot was quick to state that she was prepared to party on behalf of Harold on the 1st July. A comment which caused all the pupils to laugh, as well as Miss Patel. The matron then went on to explain that Dot had said to her that she intended to *'party like it was 1999'*, which Miss Patel found hysterical but a comment which simply confused most of the residents and all of the children, including Danny.

After an enjoyable twenty-minute drumming session, each elderly resident was handed one of their own family albums to share with the pupils. Danny was allowed to pick his partner.

"Can I talk with Dot, Miss?"

"Of course, Danny," replied Miss Patel.

So he spent the next thirty minutes discussing Dot's album with her, simply looking at some of the pictures and talking in detail about others. Having done the same with Mattie and Millie some weeks earlier, he found the questions flowed easily and Dot enjoyed answering each and every one in great detail. Danny thought that old people often struggled to recall events from the past and wondered if Dot was different to most. One photograph above all others captured his imagination. Dot grinning back at the camera, sitting on a race horse, sporting diamond-blue silks.

"Wow, Dot. Were you a horse-racer?"

Dot laughed.

"You mean a jockey, don't you, Danny? Well, yes I was, for one wonderful summer. That is my most precious photograph. I'm glad you like it. Because, now I can tell you all about it!" Dot laughed, before continuing, "that's my favourite ever horse Danny... the horse that I am sitting on. And this photograph was taken in Chepstow, Wales. That beautiful horse really did have wings that day, I'm sure of it."

"So, how did you get on in the race, Dot?"

"Well, that's why it's my favourite photograph, Danny. I won! And what was extra special is that in over fifty races over two summers, it was the only time I ever did," she smiled broadly as she went on to recall the events of that day with great clarity.

"Yeah but I'm not surprised you won, Dot. Come on... a horse with wings...that's hardly fair!"

Cue further laughter from the pair.

Dot had a glint in her eye as she continued to chat with Danny, she was full of stories from her past and he was enraptured. She didn't ask him too many questions about his life at all but it really didn't matter to Danny. While other residents had dropped off to sleep, Dot simply kept going.

The funniest story she shared with Danny was that she was actually called Barbara, not Dot! It turned out that her jockeying past and tiny frame had led to her friends calling her 'Dot' simply because there wasn't a great deal of her!

"Yeah, but you don't look like a 'Barbara' to me, Dot. Dot suits you, don't you think?" asked Danny as he leant down to give her a hug before setting off back to school. They would meet again, in July.

"That was so nice, Miss," said Lucy as they climbed aboard the minibus, "but I don't think I'd ever like to be in a home like that!" she added.

"Nor me..." added Mattie, "must've been about one hundred degrees in there. I was melting! Miss, why do old people like extreme heat so much?"

"Ah, well actually Mattie, I think they like the fresh air too but I suppose they do need to keep warm."

"Let's hope for a hot, dry day for the 1st July then," replied Mattie.

Mr Stanley's end of spring term assembly soon arrived later that week. He reminded all of the pupils that the countdown was now *'well and truly on'*! The 1st July would arrive soon enough but preparations were on track.

That two-week holiday, or at least the start of it, was already mapped out for Danny. Julie was due to collect him on the Monday morning ahead of the eleven o' clock meeting with his father. The meeting was to be held in a city centre building Danny had never heard of, which was used by dozens of social workers in Liverpool. Danny didn't really care where the meeting was held, it simply just had to take place.

That weekend crawled by but the night before the meeting, Danny slept well.

A few hours later, he glanced sleepily at his phone, noticing it was 7:31am. Moments later, out of his bedroom window, he spotted Julie's familiar blue car turn the corner and accelerate up the street slowly, before parking outside the house. Danny had rehearsed and written down the questions he would ask his father but as he heard Julie's voice at the front door, he scrunched up the paper containing the questions and tossed it casually into the wastepaper bin. He didn't need a script.

He showered, changed and was downstairs within ten minutes.

"Good morning, Danny," said Julie in a bright, sing-songy voice, "so are you ready for today?"

"Danny Bowen's *always* ready!" added his mother, on his behalf.

He smiled before adding, "Thanks, mum. Good morning, Julie and *yes*, I'm ready, once I've had some breakfast!"

Soon enough, Danny and Julie were on their way. As they headed off, Danny was relieved they had made an early start and at last, he was on his way, back to Liverpool. The journey wasn't an especially long one. Possibly seventy-five minutes but as they approached his home city, he felt some of his confidence ebbing away, like sand trickling through cupped hands. As the famous riverside landmarks slowly formed on the horizon a couple of miles north of his location, he turned to Julie for reassurance.

"Julie, tell me honestly, do you think I'm doing the right thing?"

"If I thought otherwise Danny, I'd never have set off from Liverpool this morning to collect you. To answer your question further, you'll only know if it was the right thing to do later today… after the meeting. Also don't forget, I'm there with you throughout." Noticing that Danny still looked uncertain, she added, "Look, Danny, your father is in a much better place than a year ago. And, if you wanted him back, I reckon he could be a good dad to you."

Danny was a little surprised by how open Julie had just been.

"Thanks, Julie. Thanks too for being there for me today. I couldn't dream of doing this without you. I've been confident in front of mum and my friends but I am worried too but I also know it's the right thing to do... to meet my dad, that is."

"Absolutely, Danny. Anyhow, we'll be there very shortly," added Julie before they began to thread their way through the city centre traffic, in silence.

On arrival, Julie used her pass to buzz the pair of them into a non-descript building, then to a small unoccupied room, seven floors up, with glorious views of the city centre. Danny was left alone for two minutes. He took in the imposing view from the window, helping to calm his nerves before Julie returned with a large glass of water.

"Here you go Danny," she said, handing him the glass, "your dad is already here. I've had a very quick chat with him and he would love to see you, if you're ready to come with me now?"

Danny briefly hesitated, before gathering his thoughts and finally nodding to indicate that he was happy to follow Julie.

Almost exactly an hour later, Danny was first to open the car door and was buckled up, ready for the return journey before Julie was even sat in the driver's seat. She put her seatbelt on, then looked at Danny, a smile spreading across her face.

"Well done, young man!" she said, turning the key and starting the car.

The weather had been pretty uninspiring and dull on their arrival but now the early-spring sunshine had burnt through the grey, mid-morning clouds and both driver and passenger could feel the warmth of the sun on their backs.

The meeting could not have gone any better from Danny's viewpoint. Nor from Julie's too!

Danny had accepted the offer of a handshake from his father as he had entered the room and at no point over the next hour did he feel that his father was trying to conceal, trick or lie to him. He had answered all twelve of Danny's questions and the meeting had concluded with another handshake.

"Danny, I've been in more situations like that, than I care to remember but that was one of the most positive feelings I've ever experienced. You both listened to each other and respected each other's viewpoint. I could almost have not been there. But I'm so glad I was!"

"I knew Julie…" Danny began, before briefly pausing, "I knew after ten minutes that I wanted him back in my life. And it's my new home, my new friends and my new school that did it for me. I've had more than one chance, more than one fresh start in my life. Maybe five or six. I kept getting things wrong and people kept criticising me and writing me off when I didn't deserve it. So, if I need this many chances, then why can't a forty-two-year-old have a second chance?"

"I totally agree, Danny!" replied Julie. "You do understand that my involvement with you and your mum will now end, don't you? Now that your dad has invited you to visit him in Liverpool over half-term, this June. If you accept, which I expect you will, then you won't have me on hand. Is that OK?"

"That's no bother, Julie," replied Danny without hesitation. "I'm gonna meet dad in June and I can't wait to tell mum, once I get home."

It had been a long day for Julie and Danny. There had been a need for Julie to meet with Rachel once they'd returned to Shropshire, so by the time she headed to her car to return back to Liverpool, dusk had well and truly arrived. Danny briefly hugged Julie on the doorstep, knowing he would in all likelihood never see her again and was mildly amused by the fact that both his mother and Julie were tearful, when they hugged each other moments later. This day, would be a day which Danny would never forget. It was the start of a new chapter in his life. He also respected and understood why his mother had rejected his father's wishes for a new beginning but Danny was ready to start from scratch – because for Danny, everybody deserved a second chance.

CHAPTER 10

The following morning, Danny made a beeline for his neighbour's house. It simply had to be Millie and Mattie he shared his news with, after his mother.

"Danny's that's amazing..." gushed Millie, "and he's even going to book a hotel for you both to stay in over half-term! Can I come?" she joked.

"Afraid not, it's gonna be *'dad and lad'* time only! He's also going to take me on a tour of my own home city. I've spent most of my life three miles from the centre but don't even know my way around the place. I can't wait, Millie. I just hope he doesn't talk too much about Everton! I think he still thinks I like football but I'm not that bothered," laughed Danny.

"Good luck with that one, Danny," added Mattie, "just make sure you don't start following the other team in red, before you meet!"

Later that week, both Delilah and Toby shared in Danny's exciting news. It didn't feel strange or wrong that they found out after the twins. After all, it was the twins who were most able to relate to Danny's situation and they'd shown their true colours in supporting him so well.

Over the course of the remaining week, away from family and friends, he did ponder a number of questions.

Why was it that things were appearing to turn out so well for him? Was he deserving of this good fortune? Was he due some bad luck? Would his relationship with the twins sour?

The more he considered these unanswerable questions,

the more often he came back to the same starting point.

That figure in the loft. Was she playing a part, an unseen role in Danny's life? And if she was, why would she?

And again, Danny would come full circle. All he knew was that he was convinced he had seen the ghost, was unafraid of her and that he felt there was some sort of connection between the two of them.

Had he already helped her? Or was there more he needed to do for her?

Again... questions.

His one overriding wish was that he hoped, one day, that their paths would cross once more. Having said that, Danny still figured that it made more sense to continue to keep this secret, just that. His secret. Mr Stanley had clearly done the same and Danny wasn't prepared to risk being laughed at or ridiculed if he was to share this experience with others.

With the clocks having been wound forward, Danny enjoyed the additional daylight and freedom it afforded, for the rest of the holiday. He had started to explore further afield and developed his appreciation for the countryside in and around Northernvale. He enjoyed the quieter pace of life, the winding country tracks to cycle along, the woodlands to explore and conquer, and all with his friends.

"So, you're telling me you have done all of your homework, Danny?" asked his mother, the evening before the start of the summer term.

"Yeah, all done mum. I did it in the first week. Anyway, Miss said we'll all get more homework in the next couple of weeks, cos of SATs."

As Danny returned for his very last term at Northernvale, his thoughts were elsewhere. In just five weeks, he was due to spend time away with his dad. Miss Patel was delighted to hear of further positive news in Danny's life. And, as good news tends to, it travelled quickly.

"Danny, I've heard about you meeting with your dad and that you'll be meeting him again in June. Wonderful news."

"How come you know, Mr Stanley? I was coming to find you, so that I could tell you," Danny replied.

"Ah well, Mrs Owen moves quicker – she couldn't wait to tell me. In fact, she was busy telling all the staff when I left the staff room a few moments ago!" laughed Mr Stanley. Danny smiled in response and told Mr Stanley that he may as well leave it to Mrs Owen to tell everybody then.

As April turned into May, the preparations for the big day continued uninterrupted. Spring was very much in control, from new-born cattle in nearby fields to the vibrant colourful flowers emerging from the school's planting beds. Mr Stanley was on a mission to spot the first returning house martins, winging their way back to the UK ahead of the summer, from warmer climes on the African continent.

"Just imagine being one of those birds!" Mr Stanley had said in assembly. So, Danny tried to imagine. But how could such a tiny creature be capable of such an astounding feat? And as they did arrive in such great numbers, Danny wondered if they had flown from as far south as West Africa. The home of his beloved djembe drum. He liked to think that they too, had heard the mesmeric, hypnotic beat of that drum, when setting off on their travels.

Talking of drumming matters, Danny and his class mates were now hugely accomplished drummers. They had enjoyed performing to all of the school's governors on one afternoon. Even *'Stanners'* had remembered his cue this time. The class, thanks to Danny, had now mastered five different drumming pieces and every member of the school community were impressed with the class.

The following week was an altogether quieter affair, with the arrival of the SATs for the year 6 pupils. They applied themselves well but Danny and his peers simply regarded them as an unwelcome pause to the 1st July preparations.

The short-half term entered its final week with Danny finding it a little trickier to focus in school. Even though he had no doubts that meeting his father was the right thing to do, the fact it was just around the corner did make him re-examine his decision.

However, as school broke up for the half-term later that week, Danny took the opportunity to seek reassurance from his mother, that he was making the right choice.

"Of course you are Danny and I think you know that too. I've spoken to your dad. You and I will get the train to Lime Street Station on Monday and I will meet you at the same station on the Wednesday morning, before we come back home. Your dad has booked a lovely hotel on the docks for the two nights. You have your phone and I will have mine. You can text or call at any point. In fact, I expect you to do so!"

So that was that. The day before Danny's departure, he spent his time in the company of the twins. Idle chatter with Mattie and Millie was the perfect way of preparing for the following day. Danny had reflected on the fact that it had been almost exactly a year since the rushed and frantic move, from Liverpool to Shropshire.

"There you go..." began Millie, "so much can change in a year and I know you'll have an amazing time in Liverpool."

Packing, for a trip of any length, was not one of Danny Bowen's strong points! So later that evening, it was his mum who did all the hard work, all the preparation to ensure that he was ready for his early-morning wake-up call.

"Will you actually speak to dad, mum? I mean once you drop me off, cos you'll obviously see him."

"Well of course I will, Danny. It would be a little odd if I didn't," she offered by way of reply, as she packed Danny's pyjamas and toiletries bag. "I think I've got fifteen minutes before I need to catch the train back here, so not a lot of time but enough for a quick conversation. But having said that, I've not got too much to say to your father, Danny!"

There was no response from Danny, so his mum took the opportunity to remind him it was nine o' clock and time for bed.

Danny's phone burst into life, piercing the early-morning silence of his bedroom. A lazy arm stretched out from deep under the duvet and fumbled clumsily for the 'snooze' button. As he flipped his pillow over to the cooler side and settled back to sleep, he quickly realised that this wasn't just any other day! He rose quickly and assumed a sitting position in his bed before rubbing the sleep from his eyes. His day – as well as his dad's day – had finally arrived. As he drew the bedroom curtains back, he was greeted by a beautiful, cloudless blue sky.

The day had started well. Very well indeed.

"Good morning, Danny," came the friendly voice from the other side of the door, which was ever-so-slightly ajar. "Kettle's boiling but no biscuits so early in the day, I'm afraid," added his mother.

"See you in five, then," he replied, whilst heading off for a shower. His mother smiled and considered that her son had always struggled with small amounts of time. A *'Danny Bowen Shower'* was at least a fifteen-minute affair, certainly never five.

Within forty-five minutes they were on the train, heading north. It was a journey of no more than sixty minutes but still enough time for quiet contemplation for Danny and his mother. The silence was broken some forty minutes or so into the journey as they pulled into Runcorn Station.

"Hey Danny, did you know Runcorn is where your dad's from? We met here, maybe sixteen or seventeen years ago now. We even lived here for twelve months, long before you were born. It's a grand old town but it seems like a lifetime ago now."

"Actually, more than one of my lifetimes, mum," replied Danny, "I like where we live now. Do you?"

"Absolutely," she agreed, "in fact, I think I'd happily settle in Shropshire for many years to come, Danny."

The conversation ceased as the train pulled clear of the platform.

In little more than twenty minutes, they were slowing down as they approached 'Platform 2' at Lime Street Station, having hurtled through the southern suburbs of Liverpool. Danny was unsure as to whether he'd ever visited Lime Street before, as was his mother too. All the more reason why Danny was taken aback by the hustle and bustle of each of the numerous platforms; the busy and hurried nature of the travelling public as well as the noisy announcements and bamboozling array of flashing electronic displays, anchored to the roof and beams of the historic station.

"Wow, it's massive! Where are we meeting dad, mum?"

"Well actually, that looks like him there – at the end of the platform, Danny," replied his mother, pointing directly ahead of them.

Sure enough, it was Danny's father, standing alone – smartly dressed and sporting a welcoming smile. Danny stepped ahead of his mother and as the two met again, his father also stepped towards his son, before they warmly shook hands.

"That's a well-packed bag, Danny. Did your mum help you?"

"Well actually, I packed and Danny watched," interrupted Rachel. Danny laughed and confirmed that was the case.

"Rachel, thank you very much for bringing Danny up today. Will you be meeting us on the Wednesday morning?"

"I certainly will. Danny does have his phone too, so I'll expect plenty of communication from you," she added, as she diverted her attention back to her son.

"OK, mum. I understand."

Danny's mother gave her son a hug and kissed him on his cheek before stepping back from the pair of them.

"Take care of him, Jeff," she said before heading off in search of 'Platform 6'.

"Well, here we are, Danny. Welcome back to Liverpool. Shall we get a bite to eat?"

Although he wasn't especially hungry, he thought it made sense to agree with his dad, who Danny detected seemed a little nervous too. The pair headed off to a fast-food burger restaurant, in the St. John's Shopping Centre. The conversation between the two was understandably, a little stifled. Danny was keen to ask more questions of his father about the past but doing so, over a burger and so soon after meeting up, didn't seem right.

Seeing as it was beyond midday, Jeff suggested that they book into their hotel, sort the baggage and freshen up. Again, Danny agreed. He was also very excited to see his hotel room – it had been many years since he'd enjoyed an overnight stay in a hotel, never mind two nights!

The hotel was everything Danny could have hoped for. A partial view of the River Mersey and The Wirral Peninsula beyond, as well as sight of one of the two majestic Liver Birds, adorning the rooftop of the Liver Building.

"The views are great aren't they Danny? When you agreed to stay it had to be the Albert Dock, we stayed in. Just wait until the evening. The night views are even more spectacular," he added.

"I like that we're on the top floor too, dad. Look at the cars... the people. They're tiny!"

They both decided to explore the city centre further but with neither of them being avid shoppers, agreed that an hour should be more than sufficient. Danny had £30 spending money from his mother and his father also promised to buy him a souvenir, so at least it could be more than just window shopping. The pair were in and out of the clothes and sports shops in no time at all but it was a music shop that caught Danny's attention.

"Hey, dad, can we look in there? That drum set looks cool," he continued.

"Drums!" his dad stated in surprise.

"Yeah, I'm into drums but it's a long story, dad. Bit strange too..." added Danny, smiling to himself before adding, "I'll tell you later."

"Well that's you and me both, son. And I'll tell you about it later too!"

After spending a while in the music shop, Jeff stated that there was a shop he needed to visit and he thought Danny would like it too. Intrigued, Danny followed his father deep into the *'Liverpool 1 Shopping Complex'*.

"Da, da..." he suddenly announced, in the grand manner of a conjurer, who had just produced a rabbit from under a top hat.

"Welcome to the *'Everton 2 Club shop'*!" he announced, whilst grinning at Danny.

"Oh," was the underwhelming response from his son.

"I can see you're finding it hard to contain your excitement, Danny," his father replied sarcastically, "come on, let's at least have a quick look."

He placed an arm gently across Danny's shoulders and encouraged him through the shop entrance.

"So, you don't really like football anymore, not even Everton FC?" Jeff asked his son after a couple of minutes of perusing the shop in relative silence.

"Nah, not really dad. Not played it for ages but you don't need to worry, before you ask, I won't start supporting Liverpool!" stated Danny, noticing that his father instantly seemed to relax a little.

"Good lad, Danny. Good lad. Now I just need to grab an Everton key ring – I lost the other one I had. I'll just be a jiffy."

Danny waited patiently as his dad queued up. With 'shopping' ticked off the list, the duo headed back towards their hotel room. With more time on their hands, it was Danny who spotted and suggested visiting the *'Museum of Liverpool'*.

Resembling a futuristic spaceship, which had landed adjacent to the docks, it was a most impressive sight – spectacular even and both were keen to explore further. On entering, Danny realised it was set over three huge, sweeping floors. The scope and volume of the exhibitions, as well as their link to Danny's home city was impressive.

"I'm into History at school now, dad. It's probably my favourite subject. Used to be my worst!"

"Well, that's brilliant, so this should be right up your street, Danny," replied his father.

The pair hopped from one corner to another and from floor to floor. From *'The Great Port'* to the *'Overhead Railway'* and on to *'The Blitz'*. Danny and his dad were in their element. Inevitably, his dad gravitated towards the exhibition on the city's rich footballing heritage. It didn't go unnoticed to Danny that his father seemed to focus on just one half – the blue half – of this footballing story. But it was the varied and world-renowned musical story of the city that really caught Danny's eye.

"Hey dad, let's look at this. I told you about me liking drums."

Danny was especially impressed by the city's influence on the music scene for the previous sixty years or so. He took the opportunity to explain his recent fascination and love for drumming.

"So, you're leading the drumming lessons in class, Danny. That's amazing, I'm so proud of you."

"But, dad, you mentioned drumming earlier. So, you like drums too?"

His father went on to explain that, as a teenager, he'd played the drums in a band made up of school mates.

"But don't get too excited, Danny. I don't feature in this musical exhibition!"

They both laughed but Danny's dad was extremely proud, once again, when Danny explained he would be leading the drumming and musical procession on the 1st July.

Danny had even toyed with the idea of mentioning the ghost but had resisted. He had though mentioned everything but the ghost and was later relieved that he had left it there.

"D'you know what, Danny? Why don't we go and look around *'The Beatles Museum'* tomorrow? It's next to our hotel too. You can find out all you need to about Ringo Starr."

"Ringo Starr… Ringo Starr! Who's he?" exclaimed Danny, whilst pulling a face.

"Well, let's say he's someone you could try and emulate in years to come." replied his father, with a smile.

Moving on from the museum, they headed back to their room. Danny offered to make the tea, as the pair put their feet up and recharged their batteries, ahead of the evening. As his father showered, later that afternoon, Danny took the opportunity to text his mum.

Hi mum. How r u?
Going really well here.
Enjoying it. Done loads.
Finding out about The Beatles
tomorrow. U heard of
Ringo Starr?
Luv, Danny.

Two minutes later, his phone buzzed and vibrated, alerting Danny to his mother's quick response.

Hi Danny.
Glad it's going well.
I'm tidying your bedroom at the mo.
What a mess!
And yes, of course I know who Ringo
Starr is! Who doesn't? A drummer
obviously. You'll find out tomorrow
I expect. Luv u 2.
Mum xxx

Danny had considered texting back but after placing his phone back on his bedside table, he quickly dozed off.

CHAPTER 11

"Wakey, wakey Sunshine!"

Danny slowly opened his eyes, yawning lazily before stretching his arms out above his head.

"Hi dad… how long have I been asleep?"

"Oh, only forty minutes or so. Understandable, it's been a busy old day. Fancy getting a bite to eat for tea? It's on me."

They didn't venture too far. A restaurant on the docks, overlooking the River Mersey, seemed to fit the bill. Danny enjoyed a starter, main and pudding, whilst his dad wondered how he managed to fit it all in. After settling up, they strolled onto the dock front. Both slipped their jumpers back on. Even though it was the early stages of summer there was still a keen westerly breeze blowing in off the Mersey, and further out, the Irish Sea.

They said nothing at all for a few brief moments, enabling Danny to take in the scene and reflect on the enjoyable day he had had. However, now felt like the right time to discuss elements of their shared past, so Danny took the opportunity.

"Dad, I know we spoke with Julie a few weeks ago but I didn't ask you one question I wanted to."

"Oh, I see… well what was it Danny?"

"Did you ever love mum, dad?" he asked, without hesitation.

Danny's dad laughed a little, which surprised Danny.

"Of course, I did, Danny. In fact, I still do," he replied, not stopping to take a breath.

"So then, here's my second question. Why would you

treat someone you love, the way you did, Dad?" For Danny, it was simple. If you loved and cared about someone so much, you'd never hurt them. It was a question he wanted his father to answer. This time his father didn't laugh, nor did he say a single word for ten seconds or more.

"That's so difficult to answer, Danny. It's actually impossible, without it making it sound like I'm coming up with one excuse after another," replied his father, awkwardly.

"Well, can you try please?" persisted Danny.

For the next five minutes, Danny simply listened, as he followed the path of a small boat battling against the wind and the rising tide as it navigated its way out of the docks, heading in a north-westerly direction, up and away from Liverpool. Judging by the interest of a dozen or so trailing seagulls, Danny thought that the boat was most likely some type of fishing trawler.

Danny was standing next to his father, but almost facing in opposite directions, as he continued to follow the boat's progress.

His father did eventually reply. He covered losing his job – twice; having financial problems over many years and also drinking too much, too often. He admitted being pretty poor at being a good father to Danny and not taking the responsibilities of parenthood seriously enough. He spoke of his own immaturity and selfishness and that how, eventually, it led to a souring of his relationship with Danny's mother. And Danny knew, throughout this lengthy, one-sided conversation, that as difficult as it was to listen to, his father was being brutally honest. It was that, which was more important than anything to Danny.

"Thank you, dad," was Danny's brief response once his father had no more words to share.

"Do you know, dad? I love mum so much and I will do anything for her. I used to love you too. But after you treated mum the way you did, well… I don't love you anymore. It's impossible."

"I understand, Danny," his voice slightly cracking, with regret. At this point, they glanced at each other for the first time in a while and he noticed the trace of tears in his father's eyes.

It was Danny who suggested an early night and was pleased when his father was happy to accommodate. It had been quite a day – for the pair of them.

It was another first for Danny at breakfast, that Tuesday morning.

"Fill your boots, son," suggested his dad as Danny returned to the *'All You Can Eat'* breakfast buffet bar, for a third time. Danny laughed, making a useful point that he wouldn't need to eat until that evening.

"That may well be the case, Danny but you've still actually got to move between now and then!" countered his father. The two had a final cup of tea at their *'table for two'*, before deciding on what they were going to do with their only full day. Top of the list for both was *'The Beatles Story'* Museum. Danny, especially intrigued to learn more about Ringo!

"So, they had at least one hundred and twenty-eight hit singles! That's crazy, dad. Your group didn't have one, did they?" joked Danny, soon after entering the exhibition.

"Quite right Danny. This band was the biggest thing in the 60s – a long, long time before even I was around. Grandad Len was, and still is, a big fan," he added. Danny was staggered by the facts and figures connected to the band and learnt all he needed to know about Ringo Starr.

"Do you know, dad… if I become a drummer, I'll settle for being just half as successful as Ringo!"

"So just the sixty-four hit singles, Danny. Now that would be something."

Danny's dad explained, that seeing that he now knew so

much about *'The Beatles'*, it was worth visiting a club that the band had played out of on hundreds of occasions in the 1960s. A fifteen minute walk to Matthew Street and Danny was heading down the steps into *'The Cavern Club'* for the very first time.

"Wow, this is like an underground cave, dad. Music, history and drumming – what a mix!" exclaimed Danny, whilst closely examining the pictures and information on display. The pair immersed themselves in the story and sounds of this famous venue, spending hours in there, before clambering back up the steps into the hustle and bustle of Matthew Street.

Approaching 3pm and twenty-five degrees centigrade, on a sunny June afternoon, Danny and his dad retreated to a smoothie bar for a welcome and refreshing break. After refuelling, it was a whistle-stop tour of the city on an open-top, double-decker tourist bus, ahead of a couple of revolutions on the big wheel back at the docks. Danny loved the fact he could clearly see off to Southport in one direction, Cheshire in the other and even off in to North Wales, when casting his eye westward.

Both being creatures of habit, they then headed back to the hotel room to relax before eating out at the same restaurant as the previous evening.

"I'll have exactly the same as yesterday evening, please," stated Danny enthusiastically, ahead of ordering their meals. The conversation flowed as naturally as the Mersey did outside the restaurant window. There was no awkwardness or suspicion on the part of Danny. His trust in his father had been further repaired after the previous evening's conversation, coupled with another unforgettable day out. The more Danny pondered his future, the more he could see his father playing a part in it. Again, after settling the bill, they stood in precisely the same spot on the dockside as the previous evening, both looking westward, side by side.

This time though, a much larger ship, made up of three decks, was navigating its way into the dock. Danny wondered where the passengers on board originated from and whether this was their final destination. The two spoke for an hour or more and about nothing in particular. The sea breeze was warmer too, and gentler than the previous evening. This encouraged Danny and his father to stay out for so much longer before finally heading back to their hotel room for their final night together.

As Danny woke, on that Wednesday morning, he felt a degree of sadness that this was his last morning in Liverpool with his father. They were due to meet back at the train station at midday.

As tradition dictated, they breakfasted in style but it was just the two visits to the buffet for Danny on this occasion. He accepted that a lunchtime departure, couldn't possibly justify a third visit. His father was in agreement. After packing up their belongings they checked out of the hotel, before strolling back into the city centre.

"What do you fancy doing now, Danny? We've got about an hour to kill."

Danny knew exactly what he wanted to do but needed to be quite cunning in how he went about it.

"Well actually, dad, I want to get something for mum and seeing as I'm eleven I'd like to go on my own. Can we meet back here in twenty minutes?"

His father hesitated before agreeing to Danny's proposal. It suited him too, as he planned to buy a surprise gift for his son.

As they parted, Danny Bowen considered himself a boy on a mission. He quickly popped into a department store and hurriedly purchased his mother a light summer scarf. He then hot-footed it back to the Everton Club Shop. A cautionary scan from outside confirmed that his father was elsewhere, so Danny quickly dived in and grabbed a pair of size 10 Everton slippers. He opted for the 'gift-wrapped' service and was relieved to be left with £2.50 change. Present-wrapping, unlike drumming, wasn't one of Danny's natural areas of strength so the additional service he opted for was well worth the extra cost and three minute wait. Perfectly wrapped, in club-crested gift paper, Danny placed it neatly at the bottom of the department store paper bag.

Mission accomplished, Danny even arrived back at the meeting two minutes ahead of schedule. Even so, he found his father standing, patiently waiting for his returning son.

"Did you get what you wanted, Danny?"

"Yes, thanks."

I did too, here you go..." his father said as he handed over a plastic bag. Danny was surprised and delighted in equal measure as he pulled out a hard-back book, entitled, *'The Mersey Beat'*.

"There you go, son. A book to inspire you musically. A book to help you emulate Ringo and most importantly a book to remind you of our time together, in *our* city."

His dad had even managed to date the inside cover and leave a short message for Danny. It read:

To Danny,
Thank you for being brave and allowing
me back into your life, even if it is for no more
than the last three days. I couldn't be prouder
of you, Danny. Good luck on the 1st July.
Love, Dad. xxx

"I've got something for you too, dad," grinned Danny. They both smiled as they laid eyes on the Everton wrapping paper.

"You shouldn't have, Danny but I've got to admit I'm

quite excited though! Wow... slippers, and Everton slippers at that. What more could a dad ask for? Thank you, Danny."

"Why not try them on now, dad?"

"What... in the street? Maybe not but how about we grab a quick drink before we meet your mum?"

After a final coffee for Jeff and a last cup of tea for Danny, they headed over to the train station. Danny was aware of the need to talk whilst they walked. He didn't want to leave what he had to say to the last minute, for fear of not saying it at all. So, just as Lime Street Station appeared on the horizon, he spoke up.

"Thanks, dad... for the last few days. They've been brilliant. I'd love to do it again, one day, but more importantly it would be great if we were best mates again. What d'you think?" he asked optimistically.

"Danny, I can't explain how much I've wanted to hear you utter those words. There's no better suggestion anybody could ever make to me. Thank you, son!"

They hugged each other in the middle of the street, whilst others busily stepped around them. The embrace led to Danny's dad momentarily lifting Danny's feet clear of the pavement, before carefully lowering him back down.

For Danny, this trip had simply been amazing. He had stopped short of saying that he loved his father and that was important to Danny. That, if it ever were to happen, would take much longer.

Rachel was waiting exactly where she had left her son, three days prior. As they met, she kissed and hugged him.

"So, how was it, Danny?"

He glanced briefly at his grinning father before rating it *'ten out of ten'*. They all smiled.

"Thank you, Jeff," Danny's mum said. He also noticed that as she said this, she stepped forward and placed the palm of her left hand briefly on his elbow, by way of confirming her gratitude. A simple handshake and *'see you later'*, between father and son, led to Danny and his mother heading off for their homeward-bound train journey.

It was over.

Most importantly to Danny, his relationship with his mother now felt even stronger. She had, of course, been right to encourage Danny to meet his father again. And whilst Danny didn't say it to his mother, he admired her and loved her even more for doing so. She had suffered on many occasions, at the hands of Danny's father but was still understanding, forgiving and wise enough to somehow know that he needed a future relationship with his father. Danny also felt no guilt at enjoying his father's company once more.

It was the dependable Doubty twins that Danny had ensured he had informed first and both he and his mother were delighted when, the following day, Mattie and Millie turned up with a celebratory, home-made cake. Though Danny was slightly less impressed with Mattie chomping through approximately half of *his* cake within the hour! It was widely known that Mattie had an appetite to rival Danny's.

It was also important for Danny to inform Delilah and Toby before they returned to school and this was exactly what he did. He figured that anybody else interested in his trip could wait until that final half-term began. All except for Julie. Rachel took care of this, phoning her with the good news on the final Sunday of the half-term.

It wasn't long before Danny was lacing, or rather squeezing his feet into his school shoes, ahead of his last seven weeks at Northernvale Primary.

"Good luck, Danny…" began his mother, whilst leaning against the wide-open, front door, "have a lovely day in school and continue to make me proud!"

Danny simply smiled and saluted her in an exaggerated manner.

"Will do," he shouted over his shoulder as he strode down the narrow garden pathway to the gate.

That first week back at school was a quiet one. Arrangements for 1st July were now all but ready, as were the drumming skills of Wrekin Class. *'Stanners'* continued to be on his best behaviour and slowly but surely the excitement throughout school began to intensify.

Danny had also informed anybody who would listen that his ambition now, was to be a top-performing drummer in a world class band, and to be at least half as successful as Ringo! Even though his declaration was a little tongue-in-cheek, he was pleased when Miss Patel suggested it was a wonderful ambition to work towards but questioned why he couldn't be twice as successful as Ringo Starr, rather than half as successful. Determined to act sooner rather than later, Danny looked to start to put together his own band but when nobody turned up to the lunchtime auditions, he decided to shelve the idea until secondary school.

Miss Patel had also reminded the class that Diane Bailey would be visiting the school the following week. A visit which was highly anticipated by every pupil in Wrekin Class.

"This is one of the school's most important 'VIGer' – the daughter of Flo Weston – one of the school's first pupils and later, its headmistress," she had repeated to the class.

It was the Thursday of that following week, that she arrived. Bustling into class with bags of documents and even photograph albums, she greeted the children with a wave and a cheery *'hello'*. Her arrival, at 10am prompt, also put pay to the day's Maths lesson, so she had won the class over, just by simply appearing. Their guest's IT skills weren't really up to scratch, although she proudly declared that she had produced a PowerPoint display to share with the children. As Diane sipped on her glass of water, Miss Patel dealt with all of the technological matters before the class teacher turned to address the pupils.

"Well Wrekin Class, it's wonderful to welcome Diane Bailey to our school today. Hopefully we will get a real idea of just how Diane and her family are connected to our school, and of course..." she hesitated briefly as she turned towards Diane, "we very much look forward to welcoming you back to school on Friday, 1st July, as our most special guest of our one hundred. Thank you for taking the time to visit us today. Wrekin Class, can you please give our visitor a warm round of applause?"

As Miss Patel took a seat, the class obliged. Mattie Doubty even whooped and hollered but a scathing look from Mrs Owen brought a swift and timely end to Mattie's unwelcome contribution.

"Oh, thank you so much. What a super welcome. So kind of you. And goodness me, so, so strange for me to be back in this wonderful school after such a long time," she began.

For the next ten minutes or so, the class listened intently to Miss Bailey. Most of their guest's memories linked back to the 1960s. Diane explained that when her mother returned to school as the headmistress, she would accompany her to school.

"At that stage I must have been about fifteen or sixteen, I think. My mother and I would often come in, particularly in the summer holidays, where I would help out in the class which my mother taught in. It was a little different then, I expect compared to now but while she was headmistress, she was also responsible for teaching a class too. I used to love sharpening pencils, cleaning ink wells on desks, as well as putting up backing paper for displays ahead of the children returning for the autumn term. Of course, the school was empty of children, so I spent so much time in this building but never when it was full of life and the noise of children. I suppose it was a calm place, a place where my mother and I would have endless conversations about pretty much everything!"

Millie Doubty raised a tentative hand into the air.

"Yes, my dear?" invited Diane.

"When you said, *'clearing ink wells'*, what did you mean?"

The visitor smiled warmly before explaining how children used to use metal nibs, with ink cartridges, especially for daily handwriting practice and English lessons.

"When I spent those summers here, with my mother, I was able to appreciate how much she loved this school. She would never hear a bad word about this school or the children in it. My father and I used to joke that she loved this place as much as she did us two. Joking aside, maybe she actually did... I think the fact she stayed at Northenvale until she retired tells you everything. It's about twenty years since she passed away now but I remember she would still listen to children reading, many, many years after retiring. Not sure she even left this place."

At this point, Diane paused and seemed briefly upset and quite emotional. Miss Patel spotted this too and stepped in.

"Well children, I think in the last few minutes Diane has already explained why her mother was a most wonderful former pupil and headmistress. In fact, Diane, do you think you could tell us a little more about your mother as a pupil and a headmistress? I've sorted the computer, so you just need to click this button..." Miss Patel added, whilst indicating how to operate the laptop mouse.

"Of course, I'd be delighted," Miss Bailey responded.

She went on to explain that she had school journals, pupil books and plenty of photos, due to both her parents being keen to preserve memories of the family's time together, in the past.

"I will bring all of this back with me on the 1st July and maybe we could make a small display for all the guests, Miss Patel?"

Miss Patel smiled and nodded her agreement with Diane's suggestion but chose not to interrupt her.

Miss Bailey clicked the mouse and a faded black and white photograph appeared. A hazy image of a tiny baby, blurred around the edges and barely in focus.

"Here she is! Florence Martha Weston. Born at home, very close to this village and more than one hundred years ago."

Diane continued with her presentation, including a photo of Florence (or Flo, as she explained her mother was referred to, as a child) on her very first day at school, standing proudly outside the main entrance of Northernvale, beaming back at the photographer.

The children exchanged excited whispers as they recognised their playground behind Flo, remarkably similar, despite the passing of an entire century. As the presentation continued, in chronological order, the pupils were quietly impressed with the level of detail and effort which had gone into the presentation and Diane's visit to the school. Wrekin Class's guest went on to explain how, soon after her parents married, she arrived on the scene in the 1940s. Diane Bailey had no siblings, nor did she ever marry or have children of her own. But it was clear she had a wonderfully happy and fulfilling childhood. She explained how her father often worked abroad, unusual in that era, and that he could be absent for many months at a time but Diane and her mother always made the best of the situation and were just as content together on their own as when their father returned to the country for periods of time.

Diane's presentation continued. Click. The next picture was of her mother on her very first day of her teaching career, at her very first school. Click. Next, mother and daughter captured at a school summer fete, smiling back broadly at the camera.

Click...

This was an image which caused Danny's world to come to a shuddering halt!

CHAPTER 12

"This is one of my favourite photographs of my mother – returning to Northernvale as headmistress..." Diane's voice faded away to little more than nothing.

A figure was smiling back at the children from the class's interactive whiteboard. Danny tried to make sense of what he could see. A lady smiling back... a lady in colourful clothing... a patterned jumper... a patterned skirt too... down to her ankles... a lady with short, neat hair but bushy on top... a lady Danny knew!

There was no hesitation or doubt in his mind. A shiver, emerging from the back of Danny's neck, quickly spread - engulfing his entire body.

It was the ghost. It was the ghost from the school loft.

It was Danny's ghost.

The smile, the clothing, in fact every aspect of this photograph confirmed the obvious. Danny suddenly felt light-headed, disorientated. He felt weakness in his lower body and was relieved he was seated in the classroom. He was unsure how much longer Diane Bailey spoke to the class for, or even what else she said.

As breaktime approached, Miss Patel thanked Diane, who gathered together her possessions, thanked the class and explained how much she was looking forward to seeing them in a couple of weeks or so.

Danny had found his feet and an element of composure by this point, and as the pupils filed out he did too, making his way quietly over to his favourite bench on the playground.

He sat alone, deep in thought. Slowly peeling and chomping on a banana, he tried to make sense of what he had seen.

He knew it was the ghost. Therefore, he knew the ghost was called Florence Weston and that she was a former pupil and headmistress of the school. Two facts. Two indisputable facts. But that was where his understanding ended. Questions swirled around at a dizzying pace. Again, there was an absence of any fear but an overwhelming sense of complete and utter confusion.

As that school day came to its end, he had kept everything bottled up inside. He had tried to act as normal as possible so as not to arouse suspicions. However, on his brief walk home and throughout the evening, he was continually asking the same key questions over and over to himself. It was as relentless as it was exhausting.

What did Diane Bailey's mother want?

And how could he possibly find out?

Did he need to meet her again and if he did, how would he be able to communicate with her?

She had been a headmistress. So, did she need help from Mr Stanley and not him at all?

For the rest of that school week, these questions dominated everything Danny thought about. He was unable to focus on anything else. He even dreamt about the ghost. His mother and friends had asked him if he was OK.

He was too withdrawn, so unlike Danny Bowen. To put their minds at rest, he managed to behave in a less preoccupied manner, so that soon, outwardly, he appeared to be back to normal.

But Danny was not. There was an ever-growing sense of wanting answers to his questions, and as he started the next week in school, he was just as determined as ever to solve this complex riddle.

The week in school was a busy one – a fact Danny was

grateful for. Alarmingly, it was the final school week before the *'Centenary Celebration Day'* itself. The entire school week had been put aside for these preparations. A full-scale rehearsal of the procession on the Friday of that week – seven days before the big day – had meant Danny playing a pivotal role in the proceedings. He was therefore able to focus on the drumming across the school and for the first time, the images from Diane's presentation began to fade a little. But he could still see *his* ghost and he wanted that to be the case. He had also decided not to raise the matter with anybody. He worried, once again, of being mocked or laughed at, or worse still, being dismissed as crazy. Danny also couldn't afford to be side-tracked - his focus needed to be solely on 1st July.

That Saturday morning did deliver a welcome distraction, in the form of a letter from his father. In it, Jeff has asked his son if he wanted to spend a week in Liverpool over the summer holidays, as well as wishing Danny well for the drumming procession the following Friday. He spoke to his mother and replied without delay. He figured his father would receive his letter of thanks and acceptance by Tuesday at the latest.

"Hey Danny, have you seen the weather forecast for the whole of next week?" asked his mother, with an accompanying smile.

"No, but please tell me it'll be OK for Friday, mum!"

"Well… Friday is very much like Monday, Tuesday, Wednesday and Thursday…" she replied, as she turned her phone around so that Danny could see it clearly.

"Wow, clear skies and twenty-five degrees centigrade all week," exclaimed Danny.

"Wonderful isn't it, Danny? The gods must be smiling down on us."

Danny grinned in response; everything was falling into

place. It gave him a warm glow inside. Fate appeared to be on the school's side.

The first two days of the week were sensational. An endless sky-blue blanket from the horizon in each and every direction, acted as the backdrop for a blistering sun to shine long and hard, uninterrupted all day and even late into the evenings. It was almost too hot. Mr Stanley's assembly focused as much on staying hydrated and in the shade as it did on the celebrations at the end of the week. Summer had well and truly arrived, with the whole school community crossing their collective fingers in the hope that it wouldn't disappear just a few short weeks later, as the school broke up for the holidays.

The warmth and the colour of the week added to the excitement and anticipation for all. The Wednesday of that week brought confirmation that cameras from the regional news station would be in the school for the entire day on that Friday.

By Thursday there was still no break in the weather and all were confident that this bode well for the following day. Teachers found it difficult to keep children on task, during lesson time. Preparations had gone perfectly and absolutely nothing had been left to chance. Miss Williams had also informed the children that her grandfather, Lawrence Anderson – a former pupil of the school – had arrived at her home from his Gloucestershire care home.

On that final afternoon, a message arrived in class from Mr Stanley, asking that Danny report to his office. Danny did as requested but felt some trepidation about why his headteacher needed or wanted to speak to him. In the past, a request by a headteacher for Danny Bowen usually meant sharing bad news or informing him of a consequence relating to his poor choices. However, this time, he needn't have feared.

Mr Stanley took the opportunity to reinforce how impressed he'd been with Danny's behaviour since arriving in Shropshire.

"Well, with one exception to this…" he continued, as they both smiled before Danny replied.

"But me and Mattie are great mates now, Mr Stanley!"

"Exactly," replied the headteacher, "and that's all credit to the two of you."

The remainder of the conversation focused on Danny's role and the timings at the front of the procession.

"So, Danny. Be positive. Be yourself. Smile. Lead your peers. Play the drums like only you can and it will be the most wonderful day."

Danny grinned, stood up and walked out of Mr Stanley's office. Just before closing the door behind him he couldn't resist one final, cheeky, parting shot.

"Cheers, Stanners. You just make sure you keep the beat up and bring your best behaviour with you tomorrow!"

Mr Stanley laughed heartily and shouted, "Get out of my office, Bowen!" as Danny closed the door and returned to class.

He had a light tea that evening, his mind elsewhere. It wasn't until 10:30pm, as his mum headed to bed, that Danny did the same. He had been quietly drumming out the numerous pieces of music on his djembe drum. Three hours of practice, which in reality wasn't required, as he was as well prepared as he could possibly be. Danny was hopeful, but not confident, that he would get a decent night's sleep that evening but that was exactly what he got. Moments after resting his head on his pillow, he was dead to the world. Everything was in place for the following day.

A little more than eight hours later, Danny had devoured a couple of boiled eggs and three slices of toast, after two helpings of cereal. One cup of tea later and he was ready for the day.

"Right, have you got everything, darling?" his mother asked, as he slipped on his school shoes, flinging his bag onto his back and scooping up his djembe drum, under his right arm.

"Yep, think so. Most of my stuff is in school anyway. So you'll be in the crowd for the procession won't you?" he asked.

"Of course, wouldn't miss it for anything, Danny. Good luck. I love you," she added before kissing him on the cheek ahead of watching him walk out of the house, down the familiar garden path.

School was very different. In keeping, for a very different day. For starters, Danny spotted the television crew's vans parked outside school, as he strolled onto the school playground. He could see the cameras recording Mr Fowler talking to a reporter in his classroom – a huge, white, artificial light illuminating the classroom and shining in the direction of the teacher. It was surreal. This was it - this was the 1st of July. The weather, arguably even warmer so early in the day than any other day in that week, had turned up for the celebration too. Danny could feel its heat warming the backs of his bare legs. Shorts were the order of the day for the pupils and not just the younger ones. There was another difference too. With the exception of Mr Fowler, every teacher, including Mr Stanley were out on the playground first thing, ushering the children in with the minimum of fuss, once the start-of-the-school-day bell sounded.

"We've got so much planned today…" Danny heard his headteacher begin to explain to a younger pupil.

All classes were promptly registered ahead of being led into the hall. It was at this point that most of the pupils of Northernvale understood the scale of the celebrations that lay ahead of them. Not only were the camera crew recording the assembly but all 100 'VIGers' were seated on chairs of all shapes and sizes in four neat rows, either side of Mr Stanley. The children were facing their headteacher and guests, sitting quietly on the hall floor. For Wrekin Class (the oldest and most involved class in the day) and for Danny in particular, it was overwhelming to think that by simply dusting down those old paper records from the school loft, many months beforehand, had now led to all of this.

The school had provided name badges for all guests; who in turn, had brought pictures, journals, school reports or some form of memento, linking them to Northernvale.

"So, children, you can expect any of our one hundred guests to turn up in your class, or join you in the playground or even on the field at some point in the day. And, of course, they will join us on our procession," added Mr Stanley.

At this point, Danny made eye contact with Dot, who was sitting on the extreme left of the guests on the front row. He detected a twinkle in her eye as she waved back shyly, after Danny waved in her direction, him up on his knees in the hope she would see him more clearly. She did but then she did something most unexpected. As Mr Stanley continued to talk, Dot grabbed a pair of imaginary reigns, as if on her winning horse and leant gently forward, tugging on the reigns as though her chair had transported her back to that final winning furlong. Danny laughed, waved again and was relieved to see that Dot's miming, was as brief as it was amusing. The assembly concluded with all present singing *'Happy Birthday'* to the school before three rousing cheers nearly raised the school roof!

The children quickly filed back to classes, eager to greet their very own batch of 'VIGers'. Danny was delighted to see a grinning Dot, slowly shuffling through the classroom door and he was equally amused to see that she was pretending to arrive on horseback! She was accompanied by nine or ten other guests but made a bee line for Danny, who stood up to offer her his classroom chair.

"Danny's it's wonderful to see you again, I'm sorry if I embarrassed you in assembly just now it's just that I'm so excited, I can't believe this day has finally arrived… and what a wonderful day too!"

Dot and Danny were able to chat freely for ten minutes or so, without interruption.

"You see Danny, we have three members of staff here today but they trust me to behave, so should give me a wide berth," she continued.

"Actually Dot, I never did ask you what your winning horse was called. Can you remember?"

"Oh, absolutely, she was called Skidmor."

"Skid More!" replied Danny. "What sort of a name is that for a horse?" he asked, shaking his head.

Dot laughed loudly, once she worked out why Danny was so confused.

"No…no, Danny. S-K-I-D-M-O-R," this time spelling the word out, for Danny's benefit, "now that would have been a silly name for a race horse."

"But why Skidmor, Dot?" pressed Danny.

"I think the owner named the horse after the initials of members of his family and used part of the surname, if I remember rightly," confirmed Dot.

"Oh right…" began Danny before they heard a voice from behind them. Danny recognised it as Miss Williams and as he turned, he noticed that she was accompanied by her grandfather.

"Hello, Dot. Hi, Danny. I really hope you don't mind me interrupting but I just had to?" Miss Williams began, as she glanced encouragingly at her elderly relative. "This is my grandfather, Dot. He's called Lawrence Anderson and he used to attend this school. Actually, he was here when you were Dot. You may well have been classmates, as you're the same age. Grandad, this is Dot. But you may well remember her as Barbara Morrow?" she added.

"You've told me this already, Audrey. And I told you I don't know this lady!" replied Lawrence, curtly. An uneasy silence descended on all four of them and was most keenly felt by Danny and Miss Williams.

Meanwhile, Dot wore a perplexed look on her face. Slowly but surely, this changed into a semblance of a knowing smile and only a few short seconds later it had transformed into the broadest of smiles.

"Well, I don't believe it, I certainly know you... if it isn't none other than *'Lanky Larry!'* It must be almost eighty years since I saw you and you've barely changed, Larry."

With the exception of Lawrence, everybody laughed, Danny louder than anybody – he loved Dot's sense of humour. Dot slowly and deliberately leant towards Lawrence, placing her hand on the top of his. But, at least now, his eyes were firmly fixed on Dot. Very recent history repeated itself. A look of confusion made way for a more thoughtful expression from Lawrence. He cleared his throat, ready to speak.

"Barbara? Barbara... the butcher's daughter?" he continued.

Dot almost jumped clean out of Danny's chair in sheer excitement.

"That's it, Larry... you've got it... you've got it!" she shouted. This time Lawrence laughed with Dot, then they hugged. Miss Williams felt a wave of emotion, so stepped away to observe from a distance, as did Danny. Fifteen minutes later, they were still deep in conversation, exchanging stories and filling in the gaps of the previous seven or eight decades.

"Do you know, Danny. This is exactly what today is all about. Memories shared and reuniting old friends." The pair continued to look on, observing a couple of school friends catching up, back in the building where it had all began.

Of course, some of Dot and Larry's shared stories were tinged with sadness, none more so than when Dot explained how their mutual friend, Harold, had been so close to joining them on such a special day. Larry smiled though, and shared a memory with Dot, which Harold's name had evoked. It was one of being caught by his father, after he and Harold had spent the bulk of a summer's day scrumping apples in a local orchard.

"Hey, come on grandad," interjected Miss Williams, "we ought to visit other classes, you can catch up with Barbara, sorry, I mean 'Dot', later this morning."

CHAPTER 13

Elsewhere in school, a good deal of interest centred around the camera crew. One half of the hall had been set up as a mini-studio and a selection of guests and staff were taking their turn to be interviewed. Mr Stanley followed Diane Bailey, who followed a local councillor. A clutch of children were to be interviewed too but not Danny. Mr Stanley had asked and encouraged Danny directly, but quickly realised it was next to useless. He had explained that he could wait for his big moment – leading the procession that afternoon.

With no real structure to the morning, no maths or guided reading, the first chunk of the day flew by. The breaktime bell signalled an exodus of the building. The throngs of guests and pupils headed to the sun-drenched school field for an extended thirty-minute breaktime. Music, spanning the previous ten decades, was set up on the field to accompany the chatter and all made the most of the spectacular weather. Mattie Doubty even managed to arrange an impromptu kickabout. Year sixes versus a 'VIGers Select XI'. Fortunately, the likes of Larry and Dot didn't make the starting eleven for the visitors but their more youthful teammates still lost three-nil to the year six pupils.

Back in the hall, other school staff were hard at work. Across the hall from the camera crew, staff had quickly assembled an attractive display of photos, records, journals and keepsakes, all linked to the school and kindly supplied by the guests of the day.

As everybody headed back into the building, Angie –

the cook – was shooing the camera crew out of the hall so that they could set up for serving dinner at midday. Back in Wrekin Class, Miss Patel asked that Danny, along with three classmates, bring the whole set of djembe drums from the library into the classroom, ahead of the afternoon's procession. Simultaneously, Wrekin Class welcomed yet more guests into the classroom, including Diane Bailey. Naturally, she was delighted to see so many friendly faces and was quickly engrossed in conversation with a small group of children. Danny was relieved to be busy with shifting drums from one location to another. Because, even though he liked Diane, her arrival did bring one thought to the forefront of his mind. *The ghost*.

Danny noticed that Diane's attention was quickly focused on the drums, which by now had all been moved into the classroom. As he sat back in his seat, he watched closely as Diane continued to talk to Millie. A minute or so later, Diane made her way over to Miss Patel. Conversation still seemed to centre on the drums and moments later Miss Patel made eye contact with Danny and beckoned him over.

"Danny... Diane and I were just talking about our djembe drums. I explained how they'll be at the front of our procession today and that you'll be leading the drumming too!" smiled Miss Patel.

"Your teacher tells me how you've trained up the whole class and even your headteacher. Well done, Danny. That's some achievement!"

Danny thanked her for her kind words but was unable to ignore a strange, nagging defensive feeling from deep within. Being too polite to walk away, the conversation between the three continued.

"So, are you a musician, Danny? Did Miss Patel ask you to lead the class?" continued Miss Bailey.

"Well, actually Diane, Danny and the class's teaching

assistant, Mrs Owen, found the entire set of drums in the school attic," interrupted Miss Patel.

Despite the initial uncertainty around this conversation, Danny suddenly felt that this was his story to tell, and knowing that he knew much more about Diane and her mother, than Diane realised, he decided to tell it.

"No, not really a musician, Miss Bailey but I've had lots of practise with these drums, so I suppose I'm OK at playing them now," he added modestly.

Danny quickly went on to explain their finding, after they had located the old school records previously and how he'd persuaded Miss Patel to use the class set in music lessons. He added how Mr Stanley had helped to retrieve them from the loft, as well as his back seizing up. But no ghost. Not even a mention. Danny couldn't figure how you would go about explaining to an old lady that her mother continued to haunt the school. However, Diane's continued interest and questions around the drums kept coming. Danny fielded one question after another, whilst Miss Patel watched on in silence.

Then Diane paused, before continuing.

"Do you know, Danny, Miss Patel – you say these drums appear to have been *'long-forgotten'*, when you rediscovered them. And I think you are right. But as sure as I am standing in this classroom now, talking to you both, I know 100% where they come from and how long they have been in the school!"

Now it was Danny's interest that was heightened.

"How do you mean, Diane?" Miss Patel asked politely.

"Well, those very drums made their way over by boat from a port in the Ivory Coast in the 1960s."

"But... how come you're so sure, Miss Bailey?" asked Danny, unable to disguise the excitement in his voice.

Miss Bailey smiled.

"Because my father and I drove from Shropshire to Southampton to collect them," replied Miss Bailey.

This was all beginning to make sense to Danny now. The fact that no current member of staff knew where the drums came from, the fact that the drums looked older and authentic as well as the detail and uniqueness of the patterns on each and every one of the drums. This was confirmation too, that Danny's research skills were spot on all of those months ago.

"So, these are djembe drums, aren't they, Diane?"

"Absolutely, Danny and do know about the saying, linked to the djembe drum?" Diane asked.

"*Everyone gather together in peace*," replied Danny without a moment's hesitation. Miss Patel and Miss Bailey both smiled.

"Exactly!" added Diane.

Now all of the questions were Danny's.

It turned out that Diane's father had worked for a charity across West Africa in the 1960s. After spending a year in the Ivory Coast, followed by a year in Mali, he had returned home. By way of a gift, the communities he had lived and worked alongside in Africa, presented him with enough djembe drums for a class of children, Miss Bailey told Danny and Miss Patel.

"You see Danny, my father had explained that his wife, my mother, was a teacher in England and they felt such a gift for every child in her class was fitting. And how right they were. My mother loved those drums, they were so precious to her."

Diane went on to explain that her father returned home by plane and then six weeks later, the transporter ship with the drums on board had docked at Southampton, off the south coast of England.

"I remember it just like it was yesterday, Danny. A real

adventure. My father and I, driving down in a truck he borrowed from a friend in the next village. It took us almost a day to get to Southampton Docks but my goodness, it was worth it when we got there!"

Danny and his teacher hung on every word, as Diane talked about her love for the drums too.

"You see, my mother loved school, like I said when I previously visited, my father and I often thought she loved school as much as she did the two of us. Anyhow, she did something so special for me. When we arrived back with the drums, I was allowed to keep just one. Mum said there were still enough for the class and she knew how fascinated I was with these beautiful instruments," added Diane, pointing in the direction of the neatly-assembled drums. "I treasured that drum, so it's simply wonderful that here they are again."

Danny suddenly found himself standing up, moving away from Diane and Miss Patel.

He walked into the cloakroom, gathered up his djembe drum and approached Diane.

"I've got a funny feeling that you might recognise this, Miss Bailey," stated Danny in a very matter-of-fact way.

Confused, Diane accepted the drum.

"I found this in my loft last autumn, soon after we moved to Shropshire."

"But I don't understand, Danny," mumbled Diane, in response.

Danny didn't reply but watched closely as Diane began to inspect the drum in greater detail. Gradually, things began to fall into place and it was Diane who spoke next.

"Danny, where *on earth* do you live?"

"17, Newdale Road," came the response. Diane reacted with a sharp intake of breath.

"Goodness me, Danny. That's my old home. When I was a teenager, I lived there with both my mother and father. It has a loft space with no walls… but then, you knew that didn't you, Danny?"

As Miss Patel caught up with the conversation, Danny simply smiled and nodded before going into greater detail, explaining whereabouts within the loft he had unearthed the drum.

"This is utterly remarkable!" offered Miss Patel, eventually finding her voice.

Now, with tears gently trickling down her cheeks, Diane quickly flipped the drum over, placing her right hand deep into the hollowed-out base of the drum. She then used her forefinger to trace around the underside of the drum's rim, then, once more, gasped.

"Can you see this Danny? Look, look!" Diane asked urgently, as she carefully positioned the drum so that natural light filtered in through the drum's base.

"Can you see?" she repeated, excitedly, "my mother allowed me to carve my initials, DB, into the drum."

"DB…" repeated Miss Patel, "well, they're your initials too, Danny. You didn't do that did you?" his teacher asked him.

"No Miss, not me! Why would I? It's not my drum!" he replied.

It soon became clear to all three of them, that a remarkable sequence of events had led to Diane being reunited with a treasured, childhood possession. It was also not lost on Danny that he was, almost certainly, saying goodbye to his most treasured possession too.

"Then this is yours, Diane. But please could I borrow it for this afternoon's procession?"

Diane smiled broadly, expressing her gratitude to Danny for reuniting her with her drum.

"Of course you can, my love," beamed Miss Bailey, "and long may you continue scrambling up into lofts and attic spaces in the future."

She then stepped silently towards Danny and simply hugged him.

Before the lunchtime bell sounded, Mrs Owen had managed to inform all pupils and staff about this amazing story. The episode inevitably spread like the wind and only seemed to heighten everybody's excitement and anticipation ahead of that afternoon's procession.

As Danny sat down that lunchtime, he had a brief period of time to take in everything that had happened, ahead of his big moment. He found it hard to comprehend how visiting two lofts had led to all of this. And what's more – there was still the ghost! Despite events that morning, there was, Danny decided, no simple way of slipping the ghost into conversations later that afternoon. Even conversations with Diane. He considered that, knowing who the ghost was and the connection to the ghost's daughter, as well as the drum - was there any need to now know more than he already did?

A centenary celebration menu in the hall was followed by cakes and soft drinks, arranged by staff, taken at one very long table running down the middle of the playground. As was the case with morning breaktime, the remainder of lunchtime was spent with almost all, relaxing on the school field.

But not Danny. Miss Patel had agreed to the entire class reporting back at 12:45PM so that final arrangements for the procession could be made in good time. Despite the unexpected sequence of events, just an hour or so earlier, he found it easy to focus on the task in hand. As the end of dinnertime bell sounded, Danny and all of his classmates were struck by the realisation that this was their time. Their opportunity to perform.

Mr Stanley seemed to take an age to get everyone just where they needed to be. Wrekin Class, djembe drums in hand, were at the head of the procession. Toby had been excused drumming duties, as he was to wheel his sleeping great-grandfather around the circuit, bringing up the rear of the procession. Every other pupil was placed somewhere behind Wrekin Class but ahead of Toby. There were two crew members on camera duty, ready to go, one alongside the drummers and the other positioned some way back. All the pupils, and some staff, had donned creative masks. Conversation was at fever-pitch, excited chatter occasionally punctured by laughter. The guests were invited to line up alongside pupils, wherever they fancied. Dot and Diane joined Danny right at the front. Standing impatiently, Danny was thankful of their moral support. The celebratory banners were held aloft, the carnival of colour was ready for the off. Mr Stanley instigated another rendition of *'Happy Birthday to Northernvale'* and on the third cheer, a shrill blast of the headteacher's whistle signalled the start of the procession.

"Here we go, Wrekin Class. As usual, on my count of four. A one... two... three... four..." shouted Danny, as each member of the class raised a hand in unison, bringing it crashing down onto the top of their djembe drum.

They were off.

And what a spectacle of colour, vibrancy and noise it was, as Mr Stanley, Diane, Dot and Danny stepped forward together – a television camera trained on their every move. The rhythmical, steady beat of the djembe drums dictating the deliberate pace at which the procession set off to - marching towards the heart of the village. The initial route took them straight up past Danny's house. And there, grinning and waving enthusiastically, was his mother alongside dozens of others members of the community, all adding to the carnival atmosphere.

"Hey, Danny," shouted Diane over the hubbub, "it's our home!"

Danny nodded and smiled at his mother whilst acknowledging Diane's comment too.

They continued up the gentle hill, past the post office and on towards the village hall and bowling green. Danny took a brief moment to glance over his shoulder. The carnival 'snake' meandered off behind him for as far as the eye could see – back down past his house to the turning next to the school entrance. Wrekin Class were keeping good time and the drumming practice was paying off. The crowds also showed no signs of thinning out, in fact, quite the opposite. Each and every one – whether in the procession or not – wore grins and smiles as bright as the day itself. The procession route was to head up to the village hall car park, where they could then execute a U-turn, as the car park was of a generous size. But as they approached the location a couple of minutes later, it proved a tricky manoeuvre to pull off due to the volume of onlookers as well as two-dozen parked cars or so. Danny was still going strong, the drummers now on their second round of the pieces they had practised and learnt, when he heard a loud and familiar voice from deep within the ranks of the onlookers.

"Go for it, Ringo!" came the bellowing voice, from Danny's left.

A quick glance confirmed his father's presence. He was grinning like a Cheshire cat, waving with two broad sweeping hands above his head. Of course, Danny couldn't stop but felt momentarily euphoric that his father had travelled all the way down to Shropshire and waited patiently for that brief moment of contact with Danny. In such a small timeframe, all Danny could do by way of response was to smile and quickly raise a thumbs-up to his father, before exiting the car park. That passing moment, coupled with marching back out of the car park with the middle and end sections of the procession heading in opposite directions but no more than five metres apart, seemed to raise spirits and in turn, the noise, even further.

Danny really did now have a spring in his step, the only disappointing factor being that his mum and dad weren't stood together on the procession. However, he figured he couldn't have everything in his favour. Heading back down Newdale Road, he spotted his mother outside the house again. She appeared to have been joined by even more onlookers by this point. From his house all the way back to school, the people were three or four deep making it difficult to estimate the size of the crowd.

Just a couple of minutes later, the procession, now being led by just Danny and Dot, turned sharp right at the bottom of Newdale Road. In sight of school and just fifty metres from the playground entrance, Danny's attention was very briefly drawn back to the onlookers.

As he looked left, he was greeted by more smiling faces and enthusiastic waving. Standing just behind one group, gently smiling but detached from all around her, was a familiar face, although this time she wasn't smiling from inside the school attic! Danny was certain, even though he only caught sight of the shoulders and head of the lady, that it had to be Florence Weston. But surely it couldn't be? Surely it was his mind playing tricks on him. It was hot, busy and noisy - maybe in and amongst all of this fervour and excitement it was an easy mistake to make?

Either way, he glanced back again for confirmation but of course, there was nobody standing on that same spot. Despite these thoughts, Danny concluded that it had been Flo, especially as it gave him an even warmer glow, as the procession reached its natural conclusion.

Moments later, he was striding back onto the playground – a camera focused on the front of the procession – he made his way to the spot designated by Mr Stanley, where the march would cease. It took a full three minutes for everybody else to snake their way onto the playground. In one of the more humorous moments of the day, everybody provided an enthusiastic round of applause for Toby's great-grandad and more to the point, Toby himself! With his ancient relative snugly tucked up for the procession, he had simply slept through the entire event, whereas Toby was sweating profusely in the heat and resembled a marathon runner stumbling over the line many hours after setting off.

All the same, Toby's arrival signalled the end of the procession. Following a brief 'thank you' from Mr Stanley, everybody returned to either the school field or the school building for a well-deserved break.

Miss Patel used the opportunity to remind Danny to hand Miss Bailey's drum back to her before the celebrations came to their conclusion that day. He was happy to do as requested, handing it to Diane at two o'clock. For the remainder of the afternoon, she cradled the drum, taking it with her, wherever she went.

The end-of-school bell didn't signal an end to the birthday celebrations. Countless numbers of parents collected their children before joining everybody else on the school field. Mr Fowler's class had organised an after-school cake sale, which proved very popular and extended the celebrations by a further thirty minutes. It also enabled Danny's mother to join him.

Sitting on the school field, with a cake apiece and a cup of tea in hand, Danny was in his element. He had explained the strange coincidence with the drum and also introduced his mother to Miss Bailey.

"Well, what a day Danny and what a year too!"

"You're right mum. I can't believe how much has happened... how much has changed, since we moved here."

His mother agreed and for the rest of the time on the field, the pair simply relaxed. The whole school community had done it. They'd pulled off a party to end all parties. However, Danny and his mother had one more thing to do before heading home. They wanted to track down Dot. When they did, she was still going strong and true to her word, had *'partied like it was 1999'*!

They intended asking Dot if she was happy to still receive visits from Danny even though he would soon be moving onto secondary school. Danny was relieved when she reacted with delight at the proposal, as his relationship with Dot was more important to him than he had previously realised. It was hard to imagine never seeing her again, especially after today but now their relationship could continue into the future. Danny had found that listening to those, whose life experiences were pretty much behind them, rather than in front of them, had given him a different perspective and respect for the older generations.

CHAPTER 14

As he headed home that day, without his beloved djembe drum, he harboured no regrets at all. This day and those drums had delivered something Danny could never have dreamt of, when arriving in Shropshire just a little more than a year previously.

The following week at school, especially the Monday, brought with it a somewhat deflated feeling. Many pupils, particularly in Wrekin Class, felt that the purpose and drive they had had since the autumn term had simply disappeared. Fortunately, Danny was given one more important task by Mr Fowler. The drums had been such a success, that the staff wanted to maintain the profile and use of the drums in school. Therefore, Danny was to train up a handful of enthusiastic year 4 pupils to take up their drumming roles, once September came by again. With the drums being stored in the library, Danny spent the first half of that week completing his drumming tutorials, out of the classroom.

By the beginning of the following week, all year 6 children had visited their new secondary school for transition days. For Danny, this now held far less fear. He figured he had adjusted well to Northernvale, so could easily adapt again at the end of the summer holidays, to his new environment. Life at secondary school was now something Danny was excited by and relishing.

The *'Northernvale Talent Show'* at the end of that week provided the opportunity for Danny to lead the drummers for one last performance. As he placed the drum down for that final time, he did feel emotional - even more so than the Friday after completing the procession. Moving on from his primary school was as much about saying goodbye to the drums, as it was to his friends and the staff.

The Sunday after the penultimate week in school was spent in Mattie and Millie's company. They each packed a small rucksack, Mattie's bursting at the seams with his packed lunch supplies and the trio headed off up the Shropshire hills.

The twins led the way and two hours after embarking on their hike, they carefully set down a picnic blanket, on a westward-facing slope. The sun shone, just as it had done since June and the three of them enjoyed the splendid isolation the location offered them. As they unpacked their lunch Danny laughed, as Mattie set out an additional packed lunch in a fourth place on the blanket.

"Mattie, how do you manage to eat so much? You should be the size of a house!" joked Danny.

Millie answered on her brother's behalf.

"It's not for Mattie, Danny..." she began, "it's for dad. You see, when we were much younger, dad always used to bring us up here. We loved it, didn't we Mattie?"

"Yeah, it's special up here for us, Danny. It's just somewhere we feel really close to dad. Mum understands and because it was just me, Millie and dad who used to come up, she still let's just us two come up here on our own," continued Mattie.

Nobody spoke for a moment but the three of them simply took in the commanding views, looking westward.

"Actually, Danny, Mattie does end up eating dad's packed lunch every time! So, you were sort of right in what you said..." laughed Millie, "he brought us here because he could look out to Wales, where he was born, and that used to make dad feel like he was at home. We sometimes talk to dad too. We tell him really stupid stuff and Mattie always shares really unfunny jokes with him too," finished Millie.

Danny smiled and realising how special a place this was for the twins, thanked them for inviting him, allowing him to share in their own private tribute to their father.

Unable to stifle the next question, Danny simply blurted it out.

"So, do you both believe in ghosts?"

Another pause.

"Not really, Danny… I think being here just makes us feel closer to dad," replied Mattie, assuming that Danny was asking them if their father could be a ghost.

"Yeah, but we do talk to him a lot Mattie, so maybe I do, Danny! Do you?" asked Millie, batting back the question to Danny.

"Oh yeah… 100% I do," he answered, before jumping to his feet and challenging the pair to a race to the trig point.

As that final week at primary school commenced, Danny was reassured by the fact that he was closing in on a natural conclusion to his time at the school. Not this time would he move schools in a hurried or unexpected manner. He would leave, as his year six peers would too, together, at the end of their collective primary school journey.

The first half of that week was relatively calm and ordered until the Wednesday. The Leavers' Party took place on that evening, at 6pm in the school hall. It was great fun for all and the effort and attention to detail the staff had shown in preparing the hall that evening was something every one of the leavers appreciated. Celebrations also spilled out onto the school field for a final game of rounders.

The weather continued to treat everybody kindly and it was only that evening, as Danny headed home with the twins, that they were hit by the realisation that they were very much on the verge of leaving primary school.

The Thursday morning was taken up with the year 6 pupils in Wrekin Class preparing for the following day's *'Leavers' Assembly'*. Towards the end of the day, Danny, Toby, Delilah and Mrs Owen were asked to put the drums back in the school loft.

"Whilst the year 4s will be using the drums next year, we do want to store them securely over the summer. Therefore, they're safer back in the loft rather than the library," explained Miss Patel.

The four of them set up a human chain. Toby and Delilah collecting each drum in turn, passing these to Mrs Owen, who was situated halfway up the ladder and then finally on to Danny. His job was to dip down below the same beams where Mr Stanley's back had given way, before returning to collect the next drum. Mrs Richards had taken the executive decision to promote Danny to this role as she didn't want a repeat incident in the loft with the headteacher, especially so close to the end of the school year.

With each and every drum placed back in the dark recesses of the loft, Danny felt a pang of regret. The overriding emotion was the closing of a chapter of his life which he'd never be able to revisit. But life was all about change and adapting – it was what Danny Bowen had done so much of in his life already – so he liked to think he could do it once again.

"This is it, Danny. The last one, you'll be relieved to hear. Toby and Delilah have returned to class," explained a smiling Mrs Owen. Danny reached down and carefully lifted the final drum from the hands of the teaching assistant. He guided it expertly through the loft entrance and placed it next to the others. By now Mrs Owen was footing the ladder as Danny stepped onto the upper-most rung. As he took one step down, his mood was even more reflective. He reached up above himself, to secure the hatch behind him. And in that moment he felt compelled to glance, one last time, at his drums in the loft. As his view refocused on the hatch door in front of him, he saw her once again.

One more time. One *last* time.

Everything made total sense... her smile directed at him and nobody else. The smile warmed him to the core. The connection they had, lasted no more than a second but it was all that Danny needed. Averting her gaze away from Danny, Florence Weston, djembe drum in the crook of her left arm, beat a gentle and silent rhythm as she took one deliberate step after another.

The patient Mrs Owen – oblivious to events high up above her head – stood silently at the foot of the ladder, as Danny traced Flo's final steps. This time she didn't evaporate before his eyes like the last time. She simply walked on... and on... only disappearing once she passed beyond the very dimensions of the school loft itself.

Danny's body reacted with a warm shiver as he smiled and carefully made his way back down the ladder, lowering the hatch into position.

"Come on then, Danny, we ought to get back to class," encouraged Mrs Owen.

That evening, back at home, there were no more nagging questions plaguing Danny. Whilst there had been no dialogue, there had been no need. Danny knew he had done what Flo had silently requested of him.

He slept soundly that night and woke to continued, bright-blue skies ahead of his very last day at primary school. As he slipped his school shoes on for the last time that morning, his mum smiled.

"D'you know Danny, those shoes have served you well. We bought those last summer holidays! Now you've never made it through a school year with just the one pair before," she added. Danny smiled in return, hitched his school bag onto his back before quickly kissing his mum on the cheek.

"Next time we meet, mum, it'll be the summer holidays again!" replied Danny. His mum explained that she would, in fact, see him a couple of hours later, but he'd already walked off.

The morning in school flew by, culminating in the *'Leavers' Assembly'*, attended by all pupils in the school, alongside parents and carers of the year 6 children. As the leavers shared their memories, the very recent centenary celebrations dominated but Danny didn't go for the obvious choice.

With his mother in the audience, he talked about friendships and highlighted how, through getting to know others, he now had a strong friendship with the Doubtys.

"Not something I expected after their ghoulish behaviour last Halloween!" joked Danny. He also finished with another quip at Mattie's expense – suggesting the class get ahead of him in the dinner queue, to ensure that they were fed that lunchtime.

There was though, one more surprise for Danny, towards the end of lunchtime. Miss Patel asked that Danny report back to class. On doing so, they then both headed off to Mr Stanley's office. Familiar territory for Danny.

"Hi Danny, take a seat, please," requested his headteacher, as they stepped into his office. Mr Stanley then reached from behind him, before placing a djembe drum on his desk. A look of confusion was clearly evident on Danny's face.

"Oh... did me and Mrs Owen forget to put all the drums back yesterday?" he asked.

"No, not quite Danny, it's a strange one really. The caretaker found it when opening up early this morning. It was just sitting next to the building, minding its own business, if you like. Just seemed to appear from nowhere! Miss Patel and I assume it must have been forgotten about, what with so much going on in recent weeks. Anyhow, I know that you and Mrs Owen have already put the drums back in the loft, so Miss Patel and I would like to present it to you," finished Mr Stanley.

"We'd like you to accept this Danny. From the two of us. From all at school. You're the single most important reason our centenary celebration was such a success and we want you to keep this as a memento, especially as you gave your drum back to Miss Bailey," explained Miss Patel.

Mr Stanley then continued. "And don't tell anybody, Danny but we've even inscribed the date of the centenary celebration, alongside the initials of the three of us. We also checked this morning with Diane too. She thought it was a wonderful idea – so you've got her blessing also, so can't refuse!" laughed the headteacher.

Temporarily speechless, Danny accepted the drum as Mr Stanley handed it to him.

"Oh and we've added one last thing too, Danny," interjected Miss Patel, "look carefully, next to the initials and you should see the Bambara translation for *'Everyone Gather Together in Peace'*."

Sure enough, meticulously etched out next to the initials and date was the phrase, *'Anke djé, anke bé'*.

Finding it difficult to come up with any sort of response, Danny smiled, thanked then both and promptly left the headteacher's office - the drum cradled in both hands.

That afternoon, Danny and his classmates were able to indulge in shirt-signings, photographs and final farewells. As the end of school approached, Miss Patel hugged every departing pupil, including Danny.

"Miss, if I could take one member of staff from Northernvale to secondary school in September, it would be you every day of the week," added Danny after hugging his teacher.

"Off you go, you smoothie..." began Miss Patel, as the school bell rang out to signal the end of the year.

Danny gathered up all of his possessions, ensuring his newest and most treasured item was firmly tucked under his arm. He knew Mr Stanley was never on the playground at the end of the school day but was compelled to say goodbye in person.

So, as the class headed for the exit, Danny snuck off up the corridor to find his headteacher in conversation with Mrs Richards.

"Sir, thanks for believing in me!" Danny simply stated, offering his hand. Mr Stanley shook it enthusiastically.

"Not a problem, Danny. You know, you're a pupil I've barely known for a year, yet you're a pupil I will never forget!" he replied.

Mrs Richards nodded in agreement.

"Cheers, Stanners," replied the pupil, cheekily. "And I'll never forget how you picked this drumming business up as quick as you did!"

Mrs Richards and Mr Stanley looked on as Danny turned and began to stride away, beating the drum in perfect unison with the echo of his footsteps. As he turned the corner, the distant beat faded away to silence.

For Danny, this day represented a new chapter in his life.

As he strode on home for the last time, he took great comfort in that very special djembe drum. Those humble drums had brought peace to a lady who passed away many years before Danny was born. One very special drum had been reunited with its childhood owner. The drums had taken centre-stage at a 100th birthday celebration; they had helped Danny build an unbreakable bond with the twins and even helped find common ground between himself and his estranged father. Those drums had provided Danny with purpose, direction and ambition and helped build trusting friendships between him and staff members.

Those drums had led to new relationships, no less than Dot. A character from a different era, but somebody Danny had an instant affinity towards. Those drums had brought Dot and Lawrence together after eighty years apart but hadn't quite managed to wake Toby's great-grandfather from his contented slumber back on the 1st July.

"I'll tell you what…" Danny said, addressing his drum aloud, as he rounded the corner to his house, "you've actually done a fair bit for me, so I promise I'll never stick you up in the attic and forget about you!"

Walking down the garden path, the front door opened, moments ahead of Danny opening the door himself. He looked up to be greeted by a familiar sight.

"Welcome home, Danny," said the man sporting the Everton slippers.

Finito di stampare nel mese di novembre 2020
presso Rotomail Italia S.p.A. - Vignate (MI)